awake in CHESHIRE BAY

USA TODAY BESTSELLING AUTHOR

H.M. SHANDER

Awake in Cheshire Bay

Published by H.M. Shander Publishing
Copyright 2021 H.M. Shander

Cover Design: Eleanor Lloyd-Jones @ Shower of Schmidt Designs
Editing: PWA & IDIM Editorial
Shander, H.M., 1975—Awake in Cheshire Bay

Dedicated to a summer of broken dreams,
afternoons spent in the backyard
under the red umbrella with an iced coffee in hand.
And to the Squirrels — Duncan & Carlos and their kids,
Cedar, George & Rusty

Table of Contents

Chapter One

rolled my eyes after hanging up the phone. Cedar was laughing, I heard it in her voice. What was the girl up to?

You have a VIP coming in who'll be asking for you. His plane just belly landed here, and he needs a stiff drink.

Great, just what I needed – someone who deemed himself as special. And what did she mean when she said his plane belly landed? Like without wheels and shit? How would that even work? No wonder the guy needed a stiff drink. I bet they all did.

Sure enough, the rumblings and rumours were already flowing through the pub, the joys of living in a small town. Some said there were multiple injuries, some said they thought someone died, but they were gossiping. Someone even questioned if the storm off the coast was responsible. All of them were a bunch of busybodies. Had something bad actually happened, Cedar would've mentioned it. She worked there for crying out loud, instead she was practically giddy. Whatever had gone on, it wasn't super serious.

I shook my head and carried on with my work, wondering when this *VIP* would arrive. God, I hated those types. The ones who expected to be catered to and have people grovel at their feet, yet they tell the world they want to be treated like regular folks. All lies. But that's what men do. Lie. All. The. Time.

Putting some empty bottles into a busboy tray, I surveyed the area. Did I have time to manage some paperwork in the backroom, run a quick inventory, or should I stay out and keep my eyes peeled?

I washed the countertop for the four hundredth time and went into the back room to toss the dirty rags and grab a fresh set. As I stepped back into my life, because the pub was my heart and soul, I spotted my old friend and local pilot entering with someone completely unfamiliar.

Eric locked onto me with a slight bob of his head, and I took that as my cue to head over.

The low, idle chatter from the dozen or so patrons ceased as they all took in the stranger strutting alongside Eric. He was a tall drink of water wearing aviator shades, and a navy blazer with a crisp white button up. He looked every bit the pilot that Eric was.

Inhaling a fresh scent of the lemon wedges as I ambled to the end of the bar, I steadied myself and extended my hand.

"Hey, Eric."

He smiled and stared. It must've been tough for him as he was a hugger, but I was not one of those. Instead, he gave me a solid pump. "Amber."

"How's the baby?" I gave a side eye glance to the walking sex on a stick.

"Henry is doing great."

Eric's girlfriend recently had a little one. I hadn't yet met the baby, but there was a final bonfire for Thanksgiving where that was the plan.

"Amber, I'd like to you meet, Mr. Welsh. He was enroute from the Queen Charlotte's to Seattle when they ran into some electrical problems."

Guests leaned forward, arguably to hear more details.

I waved them away. "Back to your drinks, everyone."

Mr. Welsh put his hand out to which I graciously accepted. It was warm and soft, and he surprised me by not crushing my hand in a shake the way most guys asserting their dominance did.

"Pleasure to meet you." His voice had an accent, British or something, but it most definitely wasn't local in origin.

"Are you the pilot?" I had to know, as did the other guests who weren't even trying to be obvious in their eavesdropping.

"No, ma'am, I only passenger. My crew at airport

working. A lady – Cedar? – said you had the stiff drink."

Damn, I could listen to him talk all day, and may have to thank her later for the sweet melodic voice. No wonder the girl was giddy. "Absolutely. What can I get you?"

"Jack on the rocks." He paused in thought. "Make it two, the first go down quick." Mr. Welsh turned to Eric. "You?"

Eric waved his hand. "None, thanks, I'm driving."

"Well, have a seat boys." I turned to the crowd of gawkers. "Electrical problems. Nothing serious. Back to your drinks."

I left Eric and no first name VIP to sit themselves while I went behind the bar to pour a couple of drinks for our guest. I called into the kitchen. "Dale, can you whip up a batch of waffle fries."

It wasn't anything fancy, but it helped to take the edge off. I didn't need any drunks in the place.

Three drinks on a tray, I approached the table. A light scent of cologne tickled my nose, and I knew it wasn't Eric. Since the baby was born, he'd stopped wearing any, so it had to be the VIP. It was intoxicating, like a spicy pepper mixed with cinnamon.

I set down his two drinks and handed Eric a tall, frosted glass. "It's a Coke."

"Thanks." He took a sip.

Mr. Welsh did exactly as he said he would, he downed

the first glass in record time.

"Good?" I stared into his dark eyes.

The pub wasn't brightly lit so I couldn't tell if they were blue, brown or a dark green. It didn't much matter though as they had some kind of hidden power and they weakened me slightly at the knees. What was wrong with me?

"Very much."

"Great." So far, aside from his stunning good looks and sultry voice, there wasn't much else to go with his apparent status. Weren't rich guys supposed to be charming and sweet and polite? "I have a basket of fries coming out shortly for you."

"Aren't you going to stay a while?" Eric asked, with a hint of plea in his voice.

"In a bit, maybe? I have a few things to attend to."

Besides, I wasn't here for entertaining nor for the entertainment. However, my patrons were still glued to the guest, as if waiting for something magical to happen. Small towns were funny that way. Sure, over the summer we were packed to the brim with tourists, but this guy really stood out. Most of our visitors were dressed for the beach, Mr. Welsh was dressed for a high-pressure business meeting, and damn if he wasn't nice to look at. His top button undone and hanging open, it was a great visual.

Dale rang from the back, and I went to retrieve their order. The fries were perfect, just the right amount of crispness to them. They looked good enough to eat, and I wanted to steal one before I took it over, but I held back, placing them between Eric and our guest.

"For the munchies." I beamed.

Our kitchen didn't make anything fancy, just your typical bar food, and a basket of waffle fries were usually the go-to.

"Thank you." Mr. Welsh reached for my hand. "Join us?"

I glanced over to Eric, who shrugged. He was an excellent judge of character and if he didn't seem put off by this guy, then I guessed it was okay. My own instincts weren't telling me to run, but then again, they weren't highly in tune either. I double-checked the pub, everyone was well taken care of and anything that popped up, Caroline, my employee, would be able to handle it.

Mr. Welsh rose as I pulled out my chair, a move catching me off guard. I sat closer to Eric, but turned my body in Mr. Welsh's direction, crossing my legs at the knee, exposing a bit of leg which didn't go unnoticed. The very idea of a little innocent fun with the stranger crossed my mind and lit my core on fire.

"So, Mr. Welsh, tell me, what had you travelling across the region?" Best to decide to skip over the mechanical failure part.

Eric leaned in and grabbed a waffle fry.

"Business."

"Are you from the Charlottes?"

He shook his head. "No."

Well, this was fun. One-word answers. "Are you from Seattle?"

"No."

I tipped my head back to Eric. For real? I could maybe listen to the guy talk, but there had to be more conversation than this.

He shrugged and grabbed another fry.

"Any idea how long you'll be in Cheshire Bay?"

"No idea."

"Should you feel the need to spend the night, there are a few great motels. But I'm sorry, there's no fancy chains here." I gave him another once over. He came across as a five-star resort and suite kind of guy, none of which was available in Cheshire Bay.

"I sure whatever accommodations can be acquired will be more than suitable." He retrieved a piece of paper from his shirt pocket. "Miss Cedar presented a list. Which you recommend?"

Eric stole another fry and rose. "I need to get back to the airport. Should I..." He fumbled over his words.

"Oh, don't worry about the drinks. They're on the house."

"No, not that." He retrieved some cash from his wallet.

"Seriously, Eric, put it away. Don't make me cause a scene." I cocked an eyebrow as he knew I'd do it too.

"Thank you." He focused on the VIP. "How will you get back to the airport, or should I come and pick you up in a bit?"

It was a good question. Was the airport going to be this guy's service? That was far above good friendly island service, in my humble opinion. I waited for an answer from Mr. Welsh. Was he expecting Eric to be his chauffeur?

"I be fine. I sure Miss Ember can provide number to local taxi."

Amber, but close enough. Providing a taxi was within my services.

Mr. Welsh shook Eric's hand. "Thank you for hospitality. You very gracious host."

It took Eric by surprise. At first, he wore shock, and then a smile appeared. "My pleasure. If there's anything we can help you with, please let us know."

"Yes, thank you."

Eric waved and walked out the door.

I faced the handsome guy and tipped my head to the side as I studied him.

He tapped the paper with the motel listings. "Which better?"

I took the list from him, slightly – and accidentally – grazing my fingertips over his. It was electric. And foolish.

And cliché. So friggin' cliché. I wasn't in a Hallmark movie, this man wasn't going to ride in here, or fly as it was, and change my outlook on men. This was real life.

Men as a whole sucked, and truly all the good ones were gone. All that were left were the assholes who believed you owed them a good time if they so much as bought you a drink. No, thank you. Not for me. That's why this pub was my home. I poured everything into it, blood, sweat and tears, and as sole owner it was all mine. Since it was also paid for, no one could take it away from me either.

Mr. Welsh tapped his long finger on the paper. The nails were perfectly filed, and it made me wonder just how *VIP* this guy was? Clearly, he wasn't just a run of the mill executive, this guy was high-level. He had a crew to fly him around, not just a random pilot, he specifically said *my crew,* so he had money. He was tight-lipped too, not giving away anything with his one-word answers.

"Miss?" But his voice was soothing, and it called out to me like I was lost at sea and he was the lighthouse, pulling me in.

I shook my head from the dirty thoughts suddenly floating through my brain and stared down at the paper. "If you want an ocean view, then I would select Bay Western. I believe they have a suite on the end facing the bay."

But I could only assume as I wasn't a frequent guest.

Mr. Welsh sent me a smile, the kind to melt the ice

around my holey hardened heart, and an expression that pulled me in like a tractor beam. Oh dear. If I continued to sit with him, I was going to be in big trouble. I'd already had enough of troubling men to last me a lifetime. Best to leave him be and get back to work.

"If you need anything, flag me down." Before he had the chance to vocalize a sound, I was out of my seat in a flash, back over to the bar where I continued to watch and study the foreign man temporarily trapped in our community.

So what if he was handsome? Lots of guys were. And yes, his accent was killer. Big deal. But damn if there wasn't something mesmerizing about him, and as much hospitality as I could offer, I highly doubted it would be enough to satisfy this guy. He was light-years out of my league, and men like him were never interested in gals like me.

Chapter Two

Mr. Welsh was a man of few words and not much of a conversationalist either. Just as well. His phone occupied his attention as it rang constantly and pinged even more. It was borderline annoying to me, and the patrons in my pub would look over at him every time it made a sound too. We were just more relaxed around here – no one was glued to their devices. Probably part of the appeal of a small town with an amazing ocean view.

Since Mr. Welsh was still here, and no one had come to retrieve him, I called over to the airport.

"Hey, Cedar."

"Amber." Her voice sang out. Guess she didn't look at the display. "How's our guest?"

"Still hanging out. What's going on over there?"

"The captain and first officer are still filling out paperwork. Apparently, a crane's going to lift the nose of the plane up, and they will manually push out the landing gear so they can tow it off the runway. Should be quite exciting to watch."

"I'll take your word on that."

"How's the VIP?" If I didn't know her better, I'd swear she was wiggling her brows.

"He's eating and drinking and staring at his phone."

"Cute, huh?"

"And that's about it." I shifted on my feet and leaned against the bar, staring out into the pub at the dreamy guy. "Not much personality I'm afraid. Good looking guys never did aspire to the level of charm and sophistication."

Mr. Welsh lifted his eyes off the phone and connected his gaze with me.

Great, he apparently has super-sonic hearing. I turned around and focused out towards the open-air space on the other side of the bar. It was closed for the season, but it was one of the great things about owning my own business since I designed it and it was a hit for tourists and locals alike.

"So, the crew will be there for a bit?"

"I'm guessing. Oh, hey, I got to go. The First Officer is coming in."

I set my phone down. Was it up to me to inform Mr. Welsh? Or would his *crew* keep him up to date. I left it for him to deal with.

After I took care of a few managerial tasks, I walked

back out into the pub. Mr. Welsh was still there. I flagged Caroline over.

"Has he had anything else to drink?" I worried the way he pounded back the first drink that more had followed.

"Nope. I've checked on him multiple times too."

"Thank you." It's not like I was entrusted with his care or anything.

I gave Cedar a quick text to see if she was still at the airport.

There was a problem lifting the wing up. The plane's still on the runway.

Well, that can't be good for business.

It's not. Management is here and they said I could go home, but this is too exciting.

I typed back, giving a side eye to the VIP. *If you say so.*

Mr. Gorgeous still there?

You're engaged, you brat, and you're having a baby.

I know, I know, I know. Still, nothing wrong with a little window shopping.

Take it out on Mitch.

Oh, I plan on it. L8R.

I looked up from my phone and into the wall of Mr. Hunky. "Hello."

"Hello." He smirked. "I pay my tab."

"It's all good. On the house."

"No, thank you. I pay my own way."

That statement rang far too true for me, and it was the foundation on which I stood. "Honestly, sir, it's already been taken care of. Maybe someday you'll come back to visit."

"Never give business for free."

"Consider it a sample?" I'd long ago learned that sometimes you do need to give away something for free, it's part of customer acquisition. If they like it, they're more likely to add on to their order and buy more.

He riffled through his wallet full of bills and handed me a twenty. "Consider a tip?" He held the folded bill in between his fingers.

"I can't."

"I leave on bar." There was a mischievous smile itching to spread across his whiskery face as he dropped the money into a cup.

It could stay there for all I cared. Caroline could take it and buy herself a pretty pair of earrings or something, although I know she did great for tips. However, I also made sure to pay my staff handsomely, so they weren't dependant on those tips. It kept turn over exceptionally low and my staff were very loyal in return. Win-win for us all.

"There be issues with plane, and we needing accommodations. Point me to Bay Western?" He tapped the top listing on his piece of paper. "Is lovely day to walk."

The weather had cleared up quite nicely as it had been

threatening to storm earlier.

"Sure. Take the road out to the stop sign and turn right, following it around to the next stop sign. Then turn right and follow it to Turtle Crest Landing. Turn right…"

His face scrunched in confusion.

"You know what? Do you have Google maps?"

They would lead him straight there. I punched in the name of the motel on my phone to show him. It was a good thirty-minute walk, but it wasn't too bad. I scanned down his body and settled on his shoes. Those nicely polished wingtips were going to have a fine layer of dust on them by the time he arrived. Cheshire Bay was rustic in its approach to paved roads – as in we didn't have many aside from the main road in town. The rest were dirt and gravel, and our sidewalks weren't any better.

"Oh hell. I can drive you, then you won't ruin your footwear." The word fancy almost slipped out, but I managed to stop myself from blabbing it.

"You are sure?"

I sighed as I was anything but, however, warning bells weren't going off, so I took it as a favourable sign. "Yeah, c'mon." I grabbed my purse and keys from under the bar. "First, I'm going to turn my tracker on, so my friends know exactly where I'm going."

"Fair enough."

Yes, it was overkill, but I didn't know this guy and

there were a hundred different things that could go wrong. He could leave my phone on the side of the road and drive me to my death. Or he could kidnap me and hold me hostage. He could harm me in a million different ways.

Or he could also be a decent guy who wasn't out to get me. Sometimes, I needed to err on the side of trust.

"Truck's out back."

We walked around the front of the building, past the stairs leading up to my place. I wasn't going to mention that of course. I stopped and tapped my key fob to unlock the truck. Before I opened my door, Mr. Welsh was there pulling it open for me.

"Please, I insist."

"Okay, thank you." I climbed into it, watching as he crossed in front of the vehicle and opened his side. I pulled the mountain of paperwork into the middle and shoved my key into the ignition as he settled himself and buckled up. The truck rumbled to life, and I put it into gear.

As we drove, I pointed out the road leading to one of several lighthouses dotting the peninsula I lived on, past the school which housed grades kindergarten to grade twelve, and out onto the main road.

"This road affectionately called *Main Road,* runs all the way north on this section of the island. In the middle, about twenty kilometres or so, there's a little town called Stewart Surf. It's even smaller than Cheshire Bay, like a population of two hundred I think, but it's right on some of the best beaches in the world. If you like surfing, that's a place to check out."

"I do not surf."

Yeah, he didn't come across as a someone who slipped into a wet suit and paddled beyond the break point to ride the waves. Too bad. Surfing was super fun.

"If you continue to follow the main road back all the way to the north, follow it past the entrance to the airport, you'll end up in a larger town called Spirit Bay, which if there's anything specific you require, they either have it or can order it in from Victoria or Vancouver, although the wait times are something else."

He was listening intently, leaning closer as I spoke.

My mouth kept running off, mostly because the guy was making me nervous, but not in a bad way. Instead, I felt like I needed to share all about my beautiful village to the town's newest guest. "At the farthest end of the highway, on the absolute tip of this peninsula, there's a quiet little village called *Kung Gadalayáay*, which is Haida for Moon Bay. They have whale watching expeditions and some of the best places to watch the moon set into the ocean."

"I do like whale watching."

Finally, something. I smiled as I pulled onto Turtle Crest Landing. "It's a lot of fun, isn't it? Haven't gone in years though."

"Why not?" He tipped his head to the side and studied

me. It was a little unnerving to be such a focus of attention.

I shrugged but avoided eye contact. "No time, really. I run my own business so it's very demanding and by time the busy tourist season is over, the whales have already passed by."

"That is unfortunate."

"It is what it is."

One of several bays along the west coast was visible from the top of the hill we crested.

"The motel is coming up on our left and if you're still up for a walk after you've checked in, there's a path just behind and you can follow it along the embankment all the way over to a lighthouse. Friends of mine just got engaged there a couple of weeks ago."

"It is of a romantic nature, this walk?"

I laughed. "No, not at all. It was for them. They had their first date there or something like that. It's well used by townsfolk and tourists alike, and the lighthouse at the end doesn't work anymore, so anyone can walk up and check it out."

A lot of daredevils also got frisky there too, or so I heard via town gossip.

I drove down the hill and turned into the parking lot, stopping just outside the office door. "Well, here you go. They'll take great care of you inside."

"Thank you. You have been most helpful."

"My pleasure." I leaned on my steering wheel.

He opened the door and slid onto the pavement. "Forgive for being forward, as I do not know you, but you have plans this evening?"

I had a stack of paperwork to get through, but nothing pressing. My friends were busy and once the airport situation was under control, I was sure they'd rather go home. I shook my head.

He hung off the open door. "Path behind here, it is long?"

"A couple of kilometers, if that. Nice and leisurely walk, packed dirt though."

"If I can handle that, care to join? You can send location to friend." He pointed to the phone I had resting in its holder on my dash. It was hard to argue with his logic, and even harder to resist the charming grin on the edges of his lips. I listened for the warning chime of bells… nothing. They were radio silent. Swallowing, I nodded. "You're on."

Chapter Three

What the hell was I doing agreeing to go on a walk with this strange guy? Someone needed to lock me up and throw away the key. This wasn't me. I wasn't the type of person to throw caution to the wind and go with my gut. Every action was well thought out and perfectly executed, especially over the past few years.

I couldn't afford to be careless.

"All booked?"

He strutted over with the confidence of a thousand men. "Yes. Three rooms, and one on end. Ocean view. Thank you."

"Yeah, no prob." I kicked at a pebble in the gravel and threw my gaze away from him out over to the bay.

The sun was inching out from under the heavy blanket of clouds, peeking between the gaps. It felt like it had been days since I'd seen it last.

Mr. Welsh stepped a little closer, blocking my view. "You hungry?"

My stomach rumbled a reminder of exactly how much I was. I hadn't eaten since before lunch, and it was approaching the supper hour. "I suppose I could eat." I shrugged casually, seeing as there wasn't any harm in dining with this stranger. "Sure, why not?"

"How this to eat?" He pointed to the diner attached to the motel.

Rumours around town stated the place was the number one cause for food poisoning.

I shook my head, my curls fanning out with the motion. "I'm not one to throw anyone under the bus, but I'd avoid it. There are better places up the road."

"I follow your lead." He came to stand beside me.

"First, can I ask you something?"

He looked down on me, not because he was being rude but because he was just that tall standing next to me. I was of average height, but he made me feel short in comparison.

"What is your first name? If I'm going for dinner with a guy, I at least like to know his name." A fluttery sensation filled my stomach, one that had nothing to do with hunger.

A light-hearted laugh, complete with a tipping back of his head, greeted me. "I go by Tony to most."

"And to others?" I assessed the hesitation in his dark blue eyes. "It's okay, you don't need to answer."

"Antonio."

"Antonio." I repeated back, the syllables rolling nicely over my lips. "It's a pleasure meeting you."

For some reason, he totally suited his name, and I couldn't picture him being a Johanne or Marcello or anything else. The name fit the accent.

"I like it." The smile bubbling out of me was genuine, and I tipped my head down to hide it. Seriously, why was I suddenly reduced to a wild-eyed teenager?

He waved for me to start walking. "Where you eat?"

"Mostly at home, but there's a nice grill up the hill a bit. We passed by it."

"Why you not go out?"

I tossed my hands out to the side, narrowly missing his right arm. "It's really just a time constraint. And my friends are busy, so if I'm going to eat alone, I may as well stay home and binge the latest Netflix with it."

"I see." He kept pace, but never stepped ahead, and always walked on the outside portion of the sidewalk.

The walk uphill didn't take too long, and we arrived. A strong smell of bar-be-que made my stomach growl, but hopefully Antonio didn't hear it. If he did, he gave no indication.

"Hey, Susan," I said as I approached the hostess station. "Table for two."

She ran her gaze up and down my dinner date, and I

didn't blame her one bit. The tall guy with thick wavy dark hair, and a strong jawline was exceptionally easy on the eyes. "Patio?"

After scanning the dining room, I spun to face up to Antonio. "Do you want to eat outside? There's no view, but the stares may be less."

"Yes, fine."

Susan led the way, and Antonio's hand tenderly grazed my lower back as we wound our way through the restaurant. My breath quickened and held in my chest for a heartbeat. But it was more than just Antonio. It was the familiar faces of the locals checking out the mysterious man beside me, and then doing a double take to me. Of course, the contrast between Antonio and I was like night and day, and had I been in their shoes, I probably would've done the same.

Susan sat us near the edge of the patio, where only one other table had guests.

The rocky outcropping from the embankment was our view – cozy but not scenic at all. Definitely not much to take it, but my dinner companion had the deck stacked in that regard.

After handing us our menus, Susan disappeared, likely to add fuel to the gossip. Sometimes this town was too much to take.

A waiter, one I wasn't familiar with, appeared at our table. "Can I get you anything from the bar?" He asked

Antonio first.

"A bottle of finest red."

The waiter nodded and disappeared.

"I hope you're not expecting much in the wine department. If you want good wines, I can direct you to a vineyard a couple of hours drive away."

"I sure whatever he brings," he paused and bobbed his head, "will be suitable."

I stifled my laugh, but let it slide. I wasn't a wine connoisseur per se and only ordered a few bottles from the local vineyards for the bar. My customers all accepted that, as the majority weren't there for fine wines anyway, they came for the hard stuff; whiskeys, rums, and wild selection of vodkas. You name it, I probably had it.

"Antonio, is it okay if I call you that?" I rested my forearms on the edge of the table.

He ran his fingers over his scruff, as if mocking me with a thoughtful gaze. "That is fine."

"Great, so Antonio, what do you do for a job?"

Yep, I was going to dive headfirst and not check the depth of the water.

He mirrored my pose. "I am..." His gaze darted around enough I worried he was part spy or something. "Real estate... how do you say? ..." He paused again, enough that it had me questioning if English wasn't recently learned. "Developer."

"Oh." Well, that wasn't exciting. However, the way he dressed, walked, and talked, I would've pegged him for some corporate mogul or something way higher up on the financial food chain. "Cool. I'm sure you would see many interesting places."

"Ja."

I picked up the menu and gave it a solid scan. Even though I'd been to the Grill a million times before, I still perused the choices. And like every time before, I settled on the boring standby of a grilled chicken wrap. I was so predictable that way.

"Did you decide on anything?"

He set his menu down as our waiter appeared with a bottle and two glasses. He twisted off the cap, and I lowered my head in embarrassment. The management here didn't even spring for corked wine. Yikes. The server poured a little into a glass and gave it to Antonio, who took a taste.

"Dry, but good."

The server poured two glasses and passed one to me. "Are you ready to order?"

We both nodded, and two pair of eyes settled on me. Guess I was ordering first.

"Okay, I'll have the Chicken Caesar wrap, easy on the dressing, with fries and a side of gravy. Please."

The waiter turned to Cheshire Bay's most mysterious guest.

"The bacon-wrapped tenderloin." Antonio pointed to the item.

"Mashed or fries."

"Mashed?" He sounded unsure.

"With the works, or just sour-cream?"

He looked at me before turning to the waiter. "The works?"

"That's sour cream, chives, and cheddar cheese." I answered his questioning gaze.

"Ja, that."

The waiter nodded as he wrote it all down and tucked everything back into the pocket of his apron before stepping over to the nearby patio heater. "Are you cold? I can increase the heat."

"I'm fine." Surprisingly, I wasn't cold at all, and the temperature was perfect for me.

"I good."

The waiter disappeared back into the restaurant.

Antonio picked up his wine glass and lifted it toward me. "To new friendships."

"To new friendships." I lifted my glass and clinked it against his.

His phone rang, interrupting our mini celebration.

"Forgive, ma'am. Excuse." He rose and answered, speaking in clipped and foreign sentences.

Whatever language he spoke, I couldn't figure it out.

It may have been Italian, but it could've been Spanish for all I knew. None of it sounded familiar. While he paced behind me, I sipped at my wine.

"Apologies, ma'am."

"Just Amber. No ma'am needed."

"My captain call. The plane is adjusted."

I scanned the area, before settling back on my handsome dinner date. "What does that even mean?"

He drummed his long fingers on the table and narrowed his eyes in deep concentration. "How do you say… The plane off the belly."

"Ah, the landing gear is down now?"

"Ja." He nodded and ran his hand through his thick hair, pushing it off his forehead and exposing a hint of a widow's peak.

"And it'll be ready to fly?"

"No." He took a casual sip of wine and stretched out in his chair. "New plane arrive tomorrow. I have morning meeting in Seattle."

A new plane was arriving to pick him up? Who was this guy? And what kind of a meeting did he have warranting an immediate departure by morning? I couldn't imagine much, but thinking of real estate development, maybe he was buying land? I had no idea. As long as it wasn't here.

Cheshire Bay was a small town with no chains or franchises, and every place was locally owned. It added to the charm and ambiance of the sea-side village. The nationally known places were in Stewart Surf, or more so in Spirit Bay. My beautiful town had been untouched by corporate greed, although sometimes an influx of cash wouldn't hurt to help update the buildings. However, that's what summer was for, and tourists were always welcome.

"You'll have to make sure to have a good time here then, tell your friends to come and visit in the summer." I pressed the wine glass to my lips, chastising myself for always being an ambassador to our village. It was crazy how much I loved it here, despite the gossip mill, and small town mentality.

He ran a long finger along the edge of his wine glass while locking his gaze onto me. "Tell me, what is fun times here?"

"There is so much. Lots of trails, nice easy walks. Lighthouses to see, two working, one not. There's the wharf where the boats dock for the night or the week, and some really big ones like yachts. There are plenty of excursions and many activities to fill your time. Or you can hang out on one of the local beaches and watch the sun set."

Corked or not, the wine was hitting me as I was rambling. It was possible I may have misjudged the contents by its bottle. My glass went down fairly fast, even though I was trying to nurse it. Antonio's did as well and by time our food came around, we'd already finished a bottle, and I was spewing all sorts of little-known facts about Cheshire Bay. It should've been embarrassing, but Antonio seemed to be taking it all in.

He tapped the wine as the waiter walked by. "Another, please."

As the conversation flowed freely, my mystery guest inquired what the weather was like. Yes, we were a coastal village with heat and sunshine and ocean breezes in the summer, and more rain than snow in the winter, but there was a beauty in it all, to the point where I couldn't imagine living in a metropolis on the mainland.

Try as I may though, Mr. Welsh was tight-lipped about the weather where he was from, so I was unsuccessful in getting any personal information out of him and he was exceptionally good at dodging the questions. Too good. What's up with that?

My intuition tickled with the possibility of my handsome dinner date, who worked in development, was only taking an interest in me and my ambassador mouth to buy up land in the area. Good thing outside of town was provincial land. However, it didn't stop him from flashing cash at the locals. Damn. I needed to shut my mouth.

Chapter Four

O ur dinner ended, and the waiter appeared with the bill and a point-of-sale machine. Antonio produced an unfamiliar credit card complete with a merchant name I'd never seen before, and I've seen a variety of different cards. Even the waiter looked at it with curiosity.

"Here," I said, pulling mine out from my wallet.

"No, Ember. My thank you for lovely dinner and lovely talk."

I waved my card, not taking no for an answer, even if the mispronunciation of my name was cute in his accent. The meal was expensive, and I wasn't about to be trapped in an uncomfortable situation.

"Honestly, it's no big deal." And it wasn't since I didn't go out much, and I could afford to splurge on a meal. It had been an enjoyable one, after all. Even as he struggled to speak in full sentences, I could've listened all night long.

Antonio handed the waiter the card. "Please."

There was a strength in his voice that made me not want to challenge it further.

The server didn't even glance once in my direction and quickly swiped the card through, the beeping sounds echoing off the rocks behind the tables. He passed the machine to Antonio and asked the question that always made me cringe. "What are you two up to this evening? Going to take in one of the lighthouses?"

Thanks to a website I'd read on smart comebacks to that question, I had one ready in my pocket. "If anyone asks, we were here all night."

The server froze and stared at me. "What?"

"You can cover for me, right?" I leaned my forearms on the table, and tilted my head while I quickly, playfully, darted my gaze around.

His eyes got larger, having failed to get my joke.

Hastily, he tore off the receipt and handed it to Antonio, disappearing into the dining room. No doubt to gossip with the staff and inform them I'd lost my mind. Small towns were fun like that.

I shook my head and tucked my unused card back into my wallet. My phone lit up with three messages. All from Cedar.

Your tracker is still on.

Are you still out with him?

35

Call me tomorrow – I want details. All. Of. Them.

"You smiling?" Antonio folded the receipt and tucked it into his wallet.

Embarrassed, I dropped the phone back into my purse. "What? Yeah. Sorry. Just my friend."

"You are still safe."

It could've been a question, but I wasn't sure, and I didn't want to ask for clarification. "Thank you for dinner."

"My pleasure. You good company, and you love your village."

"Yes, I do. I can't imagine living anywhere else."

He beamed. "Shall we walk? You show me more?"

I rose and immediately, his hand was on my back guiding me out even though he was behind me. Those proverbial butterflies took flight, swirling all around. Seriously, there was something wrong with me.

We'd walked through the restaurant, where thankfully not too many people took notice of us, and back out to the sidewalk, where once again, Antonio took the outside position and we headed down the hill back toward the motel.

"Where to?"

As much as I needed to leave him to his own devices and not give away any of our town's secrets, I found myself wanting to stay with the man.

"Ever been to a lighthouse?" There'd been no change of expression on his chiseled face, so I pursed my lips together as I thought of another idea. "If you're looking for something different, that path will lead us to a nice embankment and a working lighthouse."

"Go that way." There was a tinge of excitement in his voice as he pointed to the path leading to the embankment.

We took the sidewalk around the end of the street, and I stopped to show him the start of the bay.

The sand here was soft and powdery, a little teaser to the big beach near Stewart's Surf. Those were the only two with this type of sand, aside from the private beaches in front of Eric's house. All the others in the area had fine pebbles, or rocks resembling pieces of glass. I needed to remember to give him directions to those places as they were really something to see, especially the beached with all the coloured pieces, it was like sea glass or something.

"Are there beaches like this where you're from?"

He paced beside me. "Yes, but not immediate to home. Take car ride to get there."

Hmm...my brain went wild with possibilities.

"Well, here the beaches are all around the little peninsula, and the buildings are a little rundown."

My wandering gaze tried to see the area as a developer would, and while the architecture was reminiscent of an upscale 1960's style, it hadn't been as well maintained over the years. Cracks, which I thought added character, probably looked like scars to someone who'd be more interested in tearing it down and rebuilding.

I spoke and added as much personality into how things were. "That motel, the one you're staying at? It's been run by one family, over the generations, as are most of the businesses."

Antonio scanned the area, nodding slightly.

"But no one sells. Ever." I added for effect. "The beach houses, those get willed down to the children, and the grandchildren."

The house Eric owned had been in his family for three generations, and Lily's was something like that too. Only Jesse had recently acquired a beach house in the past five years, and that was a total fluke. It was on the market less than twenty-four hours.

I stopped babbling about the area and followed Antonio's mesmerized gaze out to the sea. This place, my home, was truly a thing of beauty.

"When and if you get your luggage, I highly recommend you go check out the bay, and maybe even go for a swim. You won't regret it. It's cold but refreshing."

The bay was beautiful, a little closed off from the rest of the Pacific edge so the waves didn't crash and thunder against the shore. Instead, it was perfect for families as the little ones could splash and play without worries of an undercurrent pulling them away. Although this time of year, the ocean was a little cool, but it still felt nice. And curling up in front of a roaring beach fire was the perfect way to end it.

"See what rest of night brings."

We left the view of the bay behind, and entered the grove where the temperature dipped, but the fresh scent of pine and spruce was ripe in the air.

Fall was one of my absolute favourite times of the year, the morning and evening air was crisp, and the afternoon was warm. Not everyone enjoyed the swing in temperatures, but I sure did. Mainly because I got to experience the peak heat of the day. My shift either ended mid-afternoon or started at that time.

The gravel crunched beneath my runners as we climbed the path, and tree roots appeared to twist and run alongside, if they didn't pop up through a crack.

Antonio didn't speak, and for once, I didn't either, but I wanted to keep him talking, and not do so much thinking. His silence was a little unnerving.

"Are you a morning person?"

His lips parted slowly, and he stopped his pace as if trying to understand.

"Do you enjoy getting up before the sunrise?"

A broad smile filled his face, and he resumed walking. "Ja."

"Then tomorrow when you wake up, if you do before the sun rises, come out this way, you'll see the most beautiful morning. The mist rolls in off the sea, and the air is peaceful and serene, and sometimes you can hear a ship blow its horn in the distance."

"You have done this before?"

His melodic comment warmed my soul and sent a flood of heat over my chest. He was taking in every word, every syllable, as he stared into my eyes.

"Yeah. I'm an early riser. Always have been. Sunsets don't do much for me, but a good sunrise? It can start your day off pretty magically."

"I try to take in this sunrise."

"Oh, you must." I was so excited to share my love of mornings with someone. Maybe if I got up early enough, I could meet him. Good grief, what was I thinking? I'd just met the man.

Not paying attention as I chastised myself, my foot caught a tree root and I stumbled forward, arms flailing about.

A strong arm grabbed me by the waist and pulled me close, preventing my face from being gravel fodder. It took a second before he let me go, and I'll be the first to admit, it was sure nice being held that way.

"Thank you." My heart pounded in my chest as I gazed into his eyes, my breath completely frozen in my lungs.

"You are welcome."

I stood there, facing him for some time until I felt I was able to walk again. My knees were weak, but not from the fall.

"You are okay?"

I shook my head to clear the fogginess in my brain. "Yeah. Sorry." I put a foot or two of distance between us. "I should watch where I'm walking."

"My sister is…" He circled his hand as if he was trying to find the right word. "Klutso? That is right word?"

I nodded. "Klutzy? As in she falls a lot?"

"Yes. I catch a lot too." He chuckled at some memory. "You have siblings?"

"Had. I had a brother." I muttered under my breath and turned to walk away.

The question had caught me off guard and caused the once racing blood to drain out of my head, and with it, the pounding ceased. In its wake, a knot of anger formed. Some wounds never healed.

"You do not need to talk. I understand family dynamics."

I caught my breath but continued to climb the path and put a little more distance between us. The hill wasn't terribly steep and even in fancy shoes, my guest should have no issues ascending the path. Besides, it wasn't a long uphill stretch.

However, whenever I checked, which was every third or fourth step, Antonio was never more than an arm's length away.

"Your family, what they be like?"

"Smaller now." It was meant to come out as a joke, but

that was on me.

Antonio didn't crack a smile.

"My parents live in Victoria, in a nice retirement community, but we don't keep in touch anymore."

"No? That's sad."

Why was I compelled to tell this stranger my sordid past? What was it about the way he leaned in closer to take in all I said? Why were those eyes so intoxicating to look into and feel at peace with? As if I could share the darkest parts of me without worry? It was all a lie, I was sure. Still, I could tell Antonio the things I was comfortable sharing on social media. Besides, half this town knew anyway.

I inhaled a fresh lungful of ocean air and threw my focus out into the void, refusing to make eye contact. "We drifted apart after my brother died."

"I am sorry for loss." He wore a sympathetic smile but if he knew the real reason my brother died, it's likely his smile would disappear.

My hand flew through the air, dismissing the sweet sentiment. "It was ten years ago. I've made my peace with it."

Even if I never got an explanation, nor an apology, the pain of the memories will live with me forever. On the plus side, at least I no longer had to see the monster and be reminded of his evilness.

"Your parents, did they?"

I shrugged and covered my laugh, finally taking in the

interest flickering in the depths of his gaze. "Did they make peace with the whole ordeal? Not likely."

They had a daughter who charged their own flesh and blood with the most heinous of crimes. No, they never got over *that*.

"They live there, but they do not communicate with you, correct?"

I nodded.

"They lost two people."

I no longer cared, and it took many years of therapy to learn to let go of that pain. "It was their choice. It all stemmed from a difference of opinions, and it divided us. They stuck to their beliefs, and I stuck to mine, neither bending."

More like they thought it was impossible a child they raised could do what he did, although they had implied to a small degree it was my fault, and I should've said something to them sooner. But I doubt it would've changed their opinion on their all-star, sought-after football player who had just been accepted to a major American University on a full scholarship.

"You hurt."

"I did." Shrugging off the dull ache. "I don't now though."

And it was true. Mostly.

I no longer allowed myself to be pushed around or trapped in situations I couldn't get out of. I excelled in self-defense but learned how to calm a rowdy patron before things got physical. Oh, I learned, and I learned the hard way. That was in the past, however, and my future stretched out in front of me like the beach on the sea.

In this moment though, I was tired of dancing around it, and the ache spreading across my chest wasn't good for me. Time to push it back down and remember why I came up here to begin with.

The view.

The amazing, take your breath away view.

We made it to the top and the canopy of treetops thinned out, revealing a sky dotted with peeks of blue sky among the thick, light-grey clouds. But the best view was the one beyond it as the path leveled out. The grassy trail gave way to rocks covered in a healthy layer of moss, the path more gravel than dirt and it snaked its way through the middle of the tiny embankment of peninsula.

Antonio stopped and stared, his jaw going slack as he scanned the seascape.

I knew the feeling – the first time I saw it, I thought I had died and gone to heaven.

The Pacific Ocean surrounded us, cliffs on either side a hundred feet up above sea level. As the path followed out to the horizon, the heights of the embankments rose and fell, dropping to a modest twenty feet high out by the lighthouse. Waves crashed against the rocky outcropping, an indication to me at least, how a storm was brewing off in the distance, and the salty air had a cool taste to it.

The breeze blew across my body, and I shuddered involuntarily.

Before I could protest, Antonio had shrugged out of his jacket and wrapped it around my shoulders. When he gently pulled my hair up and over the collar, the skin at the nape of my neck tingled. Did guys like this really exist? Was I dreaming?

"Thank you." My breath barely rolled out of me.

He surveyed the scenery. "This view, it is majestic."

My smile grew in strength. "Yeah, that's the perfect word."

There was a bench nearby and I pointed to it, as I needed a place to sit. My foolish legs were turning into wet noodles.

"Care to sit?"

He waited until I sat before he joined me. "Thank you for showing me."

"My pleasure."

I leaned against the back rest and gazed over at Antonio. His face was as relaxed as his posture. It was a pleasant change from the stiff form he'd be presenting since I met him.

"Do you have anything like this where you're from?"

"No."

I leaned a bit closer and as I did, I inhaled a spicy scent

lingering on the jacket. "I can't place your accent. Where are you from?"

"It is not relevant. I here only for little time."

Was it Russian? His grasp of English was damn decent, but there was just something about his voice and inflections that highlighted how much of a foreigner he was.

His attention fell away from the breathtaking seaside view and instead settled over me. "You are very beautiful woman."

"Oh, stop." Despite my protest, a blush crept over my chest.

How many other women had he said that to? Probably oodles, and I was sure they all fell at his feet because how could you not? I was fighting my own urges to resist him, and I was typically good at rejecting men. Very good.

"I speak truth."

"Well, you flatter me, thank you." My chest swelled and a content feeling spread through me.

He reached for my hand, lifted it, and planted a kiss across my knuckles. "My perfect day because of you."

The phone inside his jacket pocket rang, and I jumped from the vibration as I was wearing it.

He pulled back the lapel. "May I?"

"Oh, yes, of course."

He was being a perfect gentleman as he opened the jacket as much as possible without taking it off and reached into the depth of the breast pocket. An involuntary groan rolled out of me as his hand inadvertently grazed my breast, and I wished the ground would open and swallow me whole.

"Ja." Antonio answered, rising, and walked towards the seaside path.

Once again, he spoke in his foreign tongue, the words low and throaty. This call was quicker and before I had too much time to allow my thoughts to drift away, he eclipsed my view.

"My crew at hotel."

It was a motel, but I wasn't about to correct him, he'd find out soon enough the stark contrasts between the two.

Our time together was over.

I'd spent more time with Antonio than originally expected and had dinner with a handsome man for the first time in a long time. As much as I had enjoyed the company of the charming Mr. Welsh, it was time to face reality, as fairytales weren't real.

My heart undeniably heavy, I sighed. "Your crew awaits. Let's get you back."

Chapter Five

W hen we arrived back at the motel, there were two flight crew members hanging out by the office. The epaulets on their crisp white shirts gave them away better than a neon arrow pointing straight at them. The smaller of the two, a female, wore the pilot uniform and the tall guy beside her was the captain.

Unsure if they spoke much English or not, I walked over and introduced myself, slowly and clearly. "Amber Middleton."

"Pleased to meet you. I'm Captain Elijah Lancaster and this is my first officer, Miss Sorcha Browne." His English was perfect, as Canadian as I was, but he had a hint of an accent. "Thank you for guiding our Mr. Welsh around. I hear you are good company."

I turned and smiled up into Antonio's face. "I was the lucky one to have someone so interested in hearing about my hometown and who let me go on and on."

Sorcha lifted a lone hard-shell suitcase with the Swiss Army logo on it. "We brought the luggage."

"What happened?" I was curious to hear the facts as it would be easier to put to rest the rumours I would no doubt hear in the bar.

"We got a lightning strike, which normally doesn't do anything, but this time, it fried our system. She's all lifted and towed off the runway. We have a crew coming in early tomorrow morning to repair, priority one." The Captain looked over at Antonio as he spoke. "Should be an overnight stay tops, although we can make the call to get you to Victoria and over to Seattle for your meeting. It would be my top priority and utmost pleasure, sir."

Antonio spoke in his foreign tongue, and I could only guess at what he was saying. Whatever it was, the stern tones weren't meant for my ears or for me to understand. Until the words *Sheshire Bay* rolled out, I didn't even figure it was anything about me.

The Captain cleared his throat and straightened himself out. "If you are sure, Mr. Welsh? We can have you back on the mainland in a few short hours."

"I good." He faced me and pointed to his jacket.

"Oh, sorry." I removed the warmth, shivering as the cold air rushed underneath the weight of the jacket.

"Need keys." He dug through the outside pocket and

passed two over. "Give me moment."

He grabbed his suitcase and after scanning the key number, searched for the flight of stairs. In a heartbeat, he disappeared.

"Is he always like this?" I laughed, hoping to break the ice.

Neither spoke. Oh great, these two were as closed up as he was, and they were all on the same side too since they all spoke whatever language it was effortlessly. The Captain broke away and stepped off to the side, typing feverishly on his phone.

Trying another tactic, I glanced around, avoiding the harsh glare from the first officer. "Have you eaten yet?"

"No," the first officer spoke but she avoided eye contact with me.

Even from the side of my eyes, Ms. Sorcha Browne continued her roaming assessment of me. I've had less invasive visits from my doctor.

"There's a place up the road." I pointed back up the hill just to hammer home my suggestion. "The Grill. It's pretty decent western food. We had dinner there not too long ago. If you prefer something more ethnic, there's a great sushi place near the entrance to town."

"Thank you, I appreciate the recommendation." The inflections in her voice said otherwise.

Sorcha was beautiful, the kind of lady I could picture

Antonio having a relationship with. They were both about the same age and there was a confidence to Sorcha I found myself envious of, that and she had the most gorgeous auburn hair in a nice braid.

In trying to keep my ambassador persona close, I spewed out a few tourist highlights, but they fell on deaf ears, just hard glares.

"I'll retire for the night and keep my eyes on things." She tipped her head to the side and locked her hands behind her back, thrusting her chest out. "Tomorrow is a busy day. Mr. Welsh must be out of here before morning. This stayover is not productive."

I inhaled sharply and scanned the upper level, hoping Antonio would appear. Clearly these two were more than just his captain and pilot, but what else were they to him? Family, maybe? Perhaps Sorcha stared because she was a former lover? I wasn't sure what her motives were, but I wasn't about to ask either.

"Come hell or high water, he's lea–"

Antonio's heels clipped the wooden stairs, and all conversation came to a dead stop. At least between Sorcha and myself. As Antonio marched toward the three of us, he spoke rapidly and with a near angry tone as he spoke in his native language. It was quick though and ended with his crew stepping back, nodding, and plastering on a weak smile.

I blinked and swallowed, unsure of what just

happened.

"Want to show off the bay?" Without another glance to his crew, he lifted his hand to me, palm side up.

Curious, and without thinking, I threw a quick glance to the flight crew who quickly averted their gaze. "Ah, sure."

Silently, we descended the sidewalk to the start of the bay. It wasn't until I could feel we were out of view before I let go of my breath. A thought crossed my mind, maybe they were more than just a flight crew, maybe they were bodyguards? After all, my mystery guest didn't have an air of a normal person, he carried himself like he was borderline royalty.

He stepped off the sidewalk and onto the sparse grass that eventually thinned and faded as the sand terrain gave beneath our feet.

"Wait." I shifted and removed my shoes and socks, rolling up the bottom of the pants. "I love the way the sand feels."

He stared as if assessing his options while he rubbed his chin. "Me also."

"Trying to experience everything we have to offer?" Our beaches were known to be top grade.

"I want to see it all." There was a smirk on the edge of his lips and a glint in his eye, which sent my heart soaring.

My breath caught in my throat, and I shook my head to clear the mini fog. "Tell you what – we'll watch the sunset tonight." I looked toward the horizon. The sun was low in the sky but with the incoming clouds it wouldn't be anything spectacular. "And in the morning, I'll ring your motel room and show you a sunrise so you can tell me which, as a guest, you think is the most stunning."

Hopefully, he was still here. The way Sorcha phrased things, it was of utmost importance he be gone by then.

"This idea I like."

We walked along the sandy beach, and I dug my toes into the welcoming coolness. It had been too long since I'd been on a beach barefooted, and a satisfied sigh escaped me. I set my shoes and socks on a large fallen tree acting as a permanent bench.

"Want to dip your toes into the Pacific Ocean?"

He nodded and paced behind me.

"I'm warning you, it'll be cool, as in slap you awake cold. But it's so refreshing."

"Show me."

There was only two ways to enter the ocean – slowly and cautiously, inching in a section at a time to allow yourself to get used to it, or to just splash in, throwing caution to the wind. Antonio seemed like the first kind, so I let a smug smile cross my face and ran into the ocean, splashing as hard as I could, relishing the cool salt-water soaking into my pants. But for once in my life, I didn't care. It was fabulously fun.

I glanced back to the shore.

Antonio stood on the edge where the ocean kisses the sand, just the tips of his toes touching. He shivered but a smile bubbled out of him. "That cold."

I splashed back over; sure Mr. Welsh had another pair of pants he'd be able to change into. I kicked a little water at his ankles and his eyes lit up with a wildness that was exciting to see. I kicked again and took off in a sprint, water jumping out of the way as I ran.

But I wasn't alone, at least not for long. Antonio was splashing behind me. I turned, not expecting him to be *right there,* and we collided. He fumbled to catch me as we both tumbled into the water.

I started laughing, despite the shocking cold tearing through my body. My clothes were soaked right through and my skin was covered in goosebumps, but I hadn't recalled a time I felt happier and freer. It had been a long while.

Antonio rolled off me and laid defeated in the sand and water. Even sopping wet, he was sexy, and his expensive shirt was soaked like a sponge and plastered to his skin, the outline of defined abs evident and on full display.

I took a look down at my own body - my shirt was stuck to me and the outline of the intricate lace detailing on my bra stood out. Embarrassed but resigned, I gazed over at Antonio, who wasn't looking at my chest, he was scanning my face.

He turned and lifted himself over me, his eyes dancing

with delight. Slowly he lowered his head, and with the softest of touches, he brushed his lips against mine. I pulled my head up and pushed into the kiss, the chill leaving my body the longer we stayed connected. His kisses were powerful, rendering me perfectly helpless to ever wanting them to stop.

Finally, breathlessly, he stopped. I stopped. Our connection was broken.

He pushed himself off me and sat in the water, and I rolled to a sitting position beside him as we stared out across the endless Pacific where the sun caressed the horizon with its own tender, yet penetrating kiss. The sky was partly cloudy, and not of the good variety. The clouds were too far away to make the sunset spectacular as they hid the faintly seen soft colours of twilight.

"Oh, the sunset." I leaned against him, shivering from the unexpected swim in the ocean.

Antonio wrapped an arm around and pulled me close, his chest surprisingly warm. "We go."

"No, not until it's done." I tipped my chin towards the dipping sun. "You'll need to be able to compare."

He obliged my weak request and took in the full sunset, which sadly, never lasted very long. Once the bottom of the disc kissed the horizon, the whole show was over in less than three minutes. And because the sky was littered with clouds, the spectacle wasn't all that amazing. On the spectrum of zero to ten, it was pretty awful. I'd seen much better, but I hadn't ever watched one sitting in my clothes while soaking in the ocean. So that was a first.

"Sunset, nice." Antonio gave me a meh sign with his hand.

"Yeah, it wasn't the best I've ever seen. Rather disappointing."

I pushed up onto my feet and became a quivering, dripping mess. So was Antonio but at least he had the decency to look sexy with his hair finger-brushed off his forehead. His clothes left very little to the imagination. I, however, looked like a drowned rat and my hair was clumped in unattractive strands. I pulled my wet shirt away from my chest and shivered as the cool ocean air breezed over me causing a whole new set of goosebumps to reform. Thank goodness the truck had vinyl seats and a good heater.

The walk to pick up our shoes was long and silent, even though we were walking hand in hand. The whole way back, I kept questioning if he had really meant to kiss me, or was he swept up in the moment? Every couple of steps I'd check from the corner of my eye to see if he was looking at me, but he wasn't. He was laser focused on the tree where our dry belongings sat.

My shoes and socks hung from my fingertips as I stood on the sidewalk contemplating my choices. Get the shoes wet and walk without fear of impaling my feet on a stray jagged rock, or walk barefoot, slowly, and mad dash to my truck once

I was on the pavement. Antonio wasn't racing to slip into his fancy wingtips either.

"No shoes?"

"I right there."

Yeah, his temporary lodgings were fifty feet away.

"Well…" I was torn on what to do. Going home was the only sensible option, but that wasn't what I wanted to do. Weird how I spent a couple of hours with a strange guy and yet, somehow, felt comfortable enough to share more personal tidbits about myself than I had with some of my closest friends. How did I walk away from that?

My heart pounded relentlessly, and my fingers tingled. Gripping my belongings tighter, I tried my best to be calm and professional. "Thank you for the evening. I had a great time."

"Me also."

I stood close, shaking like a leaf on a windy day. He unhooked the jacket dangling from his fingertips and went to wrap it around me. I pushed his hand away. "My truck is there, and I'll warm up."

"Don't go. Stay." He bent down and reached for my hand. There was so much hope in his eyes, it was hard to be sensible and say no.

"I can't." The words were out before I was able to comprehend, but the sadness covering his features was like a picture of a thousand words. "I want to, really Antonio, but I shouldn't." And if I didn't leave now, I might not ever.

"Maybe I'll see you tomorrow?" I wasn't working until the afternoon. "We could do breakfast before you leave."

"Yes, breck fest."

How I loved the way he spoke, but for my self-respect, I had to leave. I stepped back, pebbles pushing against the soles of my feet, and let go of his hand. Slowly, when there was distance between us, I pulled into myself and painfully crossed the road to my truck. My hand on the door handle, I checked on Antonio. His head was lowered, and he was climbing the rickety stairs.

What was wrong with me? Here was my chance to live a little, to break out of my everyday rut, to be with someone new and exciting, and what was I doing? Crawling into my truck and leaving what was arguably the most fun I've had in a long time behind.

Screw it. That person could wait. I needed the excitement. I needed something fun and different. I hopped out, sidestepping another rock.

"Antonio, wait!"

Chapter Six

I climbed the stairs, staring into his eyes as I stepped one higher than him, so we were standing level.

"You stay?" The dark blue eyes danced between mine, searching out the truth.

"I'll stay." My heart was pounding wildly, but it felt like the right decision.

To go home would've been a mistake of epic proportions, and I've made enough of those in my lifetime. Here was my chance to break free of my little world. Besides, it would all be over in the morning, and I'd be left with a wonderful memory.

He closed the gap between us, and wrapped his arm around my waist, merging our soaked bodies, yet somehow, surprisingly, he was still warm. My breasts flattened against him and my chest heaved as I stared into his eyes, and let my gaze float down to his sweet, kissable lips.

He did not disappoint, and the moment our mouths touched, electricity flowed through my body, joining us together in a kiss that could end wars. He lifted me, setting me on the landing. The strong hands caressed my back, and with his powerful, yet sensual kisses, he could've easily had his way with me. My body was on fire, my knees were weak, and I'd found a set of lips I enjoyed kissing and would continue to for the rest of his impromptu stay.

Until the morning sun.

"Go," he urged, and he nudged me toward his room.

I grasped the hand railing to right myself, and stepped off to the side, allowing him to come up beside me.

For a heartbeat, I froze.

What the hell was I doing? I was following a stranger to his motel room. *A stranger*.

And yet, no warning bells had been set off, my intuition locked on the grace and charm of this guy, seeing only what? What was I feeling? I searched deeper. Something whispered he was okay. It was just one night. I could be that person. I had nothing to lose.

Stepping forward, my body made the decision my mind was slowly getting around to make.

Together we walked to his room where he inserted the key and entered his 3.2 star rated room. The Hilton's worst room would rank higher, but at least there was a clean bed and a dresser with a tv on it, unlikely to get the good channels judging by the rabbit ears above. I should've let him stay over to my place.

Oh, what would my friends have thought if they knew?

He closed and locked the door, pulling the rusty-coloured curtains across the window, sealing off the limited ocean view, only because anyone could walk by and easily see in. Motels offered little privacy in that regard. On the lone chair, he draped his coat and set his shoes and socks beside it.

He sat on the bed, and unbuttoned the second from the top button, and then the third, all the while taking me in. "Come."

He beckoned with his finger, and my heart jumped another notch as my feet led me over to stand between his legs. A lingering finger trailed over my cheek and pushed a wet ringlet of hair away. "You are very beautiful woman."

I certainly didn't feel it at the moment, and beautiful wouldn't be the word either as I'd stolen a quick glance at myself while at my truck. I was a cold, shivering mess with my darkened hair plastered on either side of my face, but I couldn't deny how incredible he was. "You are so handsome."

One-night stands weren't my thing. Not since becoming a grown up at least. However, I knew this was all this night was going to be. After the sun rose, I'd never see the likes of Antonio again. I could do this. I could give myself to him, right?

With my trembling hand, I cupped his whiskery cheek,

and he covered it with his own, pulling it away to plant a kiss in my palm. He lowered my hand and placed it on his muscular chest, the steady beat of an excited heart pumping beneath my fingertips. Lifting his hand, I kissed his fingers and, with trepidation and hesitation, placed them over my covered and damp chest, hoping he would feel my own racing pulse.

"Scared?"

I looked deep into his eyes and held my breath - it wasn't fear, it was something else. Like apprehension and the sensation of things moving too quickly, and yet, on the flip side, of things moving in slow-motion. Sex had been off the table for quite some time. Days, that turned to weeks, which turned to months until eventually... Too much time had passed. Not since I'd fallen in with the wrong guy who'd done a number on me emotionally, physically, and mentally. I hadn't been ready to even think about men once I threw myself into my business. Until this tall chap walked into my pub.

"Ember?" His soft voice cut through the haze and fog, and he removed his hand from my body and linked his fingers through my trembling ones.

My throat was dry, my limbs tingled, and I had enough adrenaline coursing through my system to run a marathon but still, I shook my head. To prove I was okay, and to convince myself, I started undoing my own buttons down the front of my shirt. I searched the depths of his eyes where I was rewarded with a grin warm enough to melt my heart.

I could do this. I could be this carefree woman.

He pushed the wet clothes over my shoulders, kissing across my collar bone.

Responding, I tipped my head back and inched closer, locking my hands around his neck to stop them from shaking. It had been too long since I'd been a willing participant in the love games. I wanted him, I just needed to get beyond the overthinking part and let my emotions take over.

Slowly, Antonio ran his hands down my back and around my waist, tugging my shirt free. His fingers trailed around the belt, over to the center, where he released the buckle and unbuttoned my pants.

An involuntary shudder overcame me, and I slammed my eyes shut. A myriad of thoughts and visions filled my brain.

"Ember?" A gentle tug came from my waist, his voice a million miles away. "Ember?"

"Antonio." I opened my eyes to see him staring up at me, confusion washing over his features.

"You not okay."

My voice quivered as I spoke. "I want to be." But my feet were encased in concrete and my hands were locked behind his head. "I will be. Promise. Keep going." Once I pushed through, I was bound to be fine. I'd been able to do it before, I only needed to focus on the good, not the scary.

He stretched out and grabbed my hands, holding them tenderly with one hand while he covered my chest with my shirt with the other. "No. You not okay. We wait."

"No, I want this." But the trembling moved from my hands down to my legs.

Once things progressed a little more, I would be into it, I was sure of it. I just needed more time. More foreplay. The word lit up like an explosion in my head and a giant, body wracking shudder coursed from top to bottom. Double damn.

"Ember?" His voice like the beam from a lighthouse, called out to me through the thick fog. "I have sister." His voice softened and he moved his hands from the front of my waist to my lower back. "I caught bad man hurting her." He never looked away and held me in his eyes. "We wait."

"But we don't have time." And I wanted him, wanted him with every morsel of my being but my brain refused to shut down and let my wanton emotions take over.

"We have all the time in the world."

I lowered my forehead and rested it on his shoulders. There was no way this was real. Another guy likely wouldn't have stopped. Would've carried on regardless. It wouldn't have been the first time. My words were breathless with disbelief. "You can't be real."

Seriously, what guy was patient enough to stop? None in recent memory. Whether I wanted it or not, I was going to get it because that had been what I'd teased him with.

He rubbed my back. "I real. You real."

I captured his face between my hands, and firmly planted a heartfelt kiss on his lips, trying to rev up the carnal desire once more. However, it failed to arrive, and in its wake, there was only one path I could take. "I should go home now and leave you be."

He shook his head. "No, please, to stay. We talk. We walk. We visit Sheshire Bay. Do not go."

I was grossly uncomfortable, mainly with myself. Desperately, I wanted to cave into the rush of sexual attractions, instead I proved how much a prude I was. However, that as it was, I wasn't ready to let him go just yet, and walking around my lovely village was the perfect idea. Maybe he'd enjoy it so much, he'd come back for another visit.

"Can I go home to change first?"

A hint of a side smile formed. "Ja."

Antonio rose and flipped his suitcase on the bed, unzipping and throwing it open. It was packed with such skill, I assumed he travelled a lot. He retrieved a few things and disappeared into the bathroom.

I was such a fool. Why couldn't I give into this guy? He was so sweet and genuine, I should be able to give him my body, but my mind wouldn't shut up. Was there a pill I could take to stop the thoughts and allow me to give into the carnal desires?

I hung my head. If there was, then it wouldn't be me and it would be no different than plying myself with alcohol or weed. No, if the right guy for me were to truly come around, my mind would know it as much as my body and there would be no fighting.

Someday, maybe.

But despite the want, it couldn't – it wouldn't – be with a guy I'd just met, and not with a guy who's leaving in the morning. Even if he was a dream come true. The nightmare will always follow.

Chapter Seven

Because guys are lucky that way, Antonio emerged from the bathroom fresh and squeaky clean and smelling spicy all within the span of ten minutes. If that. I was sure most of it was having the shower run long enough for hot water to emerge.

Closing out of my messages app, I glanced up from my phone as he emerged.

"Had sand hair." He laughed, and my heart pitter-pattered with it.

"Yeah, side effect of falling on the beach." My hand went to the back of my head and tousled a bit, watching in horror as part of the beach fell to the industrial carpet. "I guess I need to shower too."

"You take us there. I wait."

"You sure?"

"Ja." He grabbed a jacket, which was a smart move as

the cool and damp October air had the power to chill a person to the bone if they weren't expecting it. A warmer layer would fight that off.

"Alright, let's go." I slipped into my shoes and stuffed my socks into my purse as I pulled out my keys.

Down the stairs we went, his hand moving from the small of my back to holding my hand. It happened so quickly, I didn't see it coming but I wasn't complaining either. We got to my truck and Antonio opened the driver door for me, pausing to stare into my eyes and trail a finger over my cheek. He leaned forward and grazed my forehead with a soft kiss before pulling back and sauntering over to his side. That smirk on his face was going to be my undoing. And maybe that was his plan.

As I pulled the truck out of its spot, I spotted Sorcha leaning against the stairwell, taking us both in. The sight of her slight scowl unsettled me, but I tried to pay it no attention. Antonio hadn't seen her, and if he did, he wasn't making it obvious.

We pulled up to my place and the parking lot was full, which was promising, it meant my pub was having a good night. I drove around to the back of the building and parked in the only open spot thanks to the sign reading '*management only*'.

"My place is a tad messy, so forgive me. I wasn't expecting company when I went to work this morning."

Man, what a day. I'd totally lost track of what time it was.

Antonio followed behind as we ascended the metal grate stairwell up to a door, offset from a wrap around patio. Years ago, I'd purchased the sizeable home and converted it into a full pub on the main floor and sound-proofed the second level to turn it into a nice two-bedroom suite, with a sweeping view of the Pacific Ocean from the patio. It was money well spent, and because the pub did well, I managed to make the final mortgage payment last month. Amber's Ale was all mine.

We stepped into the space and a familiar scent of cinnamon, from the fragrance sticks I had set around the place, warmed my soul.

I gave a sweeping gaze over the living room and kitchen. It was as horrible as I'd thought. At least the counter was clutter free.

"Please, help yourself to whatever you'd like. I'll go and freshen up; it shouldn't take me too long."

He pulled out his phone and flashed it in my direction. Countless notifications lit up the screen.

What kind of a developer was he?

"Emails and calls."

Yeah, have fun with that. Those never ended. I pointed toward the peninsula in the kitchen. "There's a charger on the kitchen counter if you need."

"Ja." He smiled and sat upon my couch, which judging from the look on his face, was not as firm as the bed he'd sleep on tonight. "You go do what you do."

Stepping away slowly, I gave the area another sweeping glance. We didn't come back to spend anytime here, just a quick pitstop. "I'll be quick."

And with that, I ducked into the bedroom and pulled off my still uncomfortably damp clothes, tossing them all into the hamper. I hopped into the shower and did the fastest clean ever, drying off a mere four minutes later. At least there was no more sand in my hair as it was currently dancing and swirling around the drain. I towel dried my hair, fluffing and scrunching it to help define the curls and brushed some powder over my t-zone to absorb the shine. Satisfied with the way I looked, I scrambled into the closet, searching for something practical and yet a little sexy, however, I spent more time hunting for a matching set of bra and panties. Mission accomplished, I exited my bedroom after quickly smoothing out the duvet on the bed, and fluffing the pillows, just in case.

Antonio was on the phone, his accented voice firm and unyielding to whomever he was speaking with. He turned around and his voice softened as a smile stretched from ear to ear. It sounded like he said *weinershen* when he hung up, but I may have been wrong. The word made me giggle.

"You are stunning."

70

I curtsied. "Thank you. Am I interrupting anything?"

"No." He bridged the gap between us, pocketing his phone. "Your place is… ahh…" He was waving his hand in circles. "Homey."

I smiled. "Yes, thank you."

"Your family?" He pointed to a picture tucked in beside a few self-help books with titles like *The Courage to Heal, Toxic Parents,* and *Healing the Trauma of Abuse*

Those books had been untouched in a while, but suddenly, I felt very exposed and vulnerable knowing he probably gave the titles a passing glance and wondered what the hell kind of person he was hanging out with.

Instead of dwelling on it too much, I focused my attention on the lovelies in the frame. "They are my surrogate family. These are my friends, Willow and Arlo." I pointed to the two older people who could very well be substitute parents, and on many occasions had been. "And this is my best friend Cedar and her fiancé Mitch. This guy is Eric, he's the pilot that brought you to my pub."

"Ah, yes. He is different."

It was an older picture, a couple years old, and due for a retake since Eric was now with Lily and her son, and Cedar was pregnant. Maybe in the summer.

"Maybe if you come back for Thanksgiving, you can join us for our annual bonfire on the beach. It's a private party, held at Eric's, and there's usually thirty of us."

"Bun-fire?" His perfect eyebrow arched.

"Yeah, you know a bonfire. Big flames, lots of wood. So much fun." My arms opened wide to demonstrate, and it had me wondering if he was completely unfamiliar with the word. "Don't they have gatherings where you are from?"

"Ja, but no fire."

"Ah, you're missing out. It's just something we do here." I shrugged as memories of summer days, warm breezes and lots of laughter floated in my head. "Where are you from anyway? You never mention anything."

His shoulders sagged. "It is not close."

"Are you from Europe?"

There was a glint in his eyes. "I can not say."

"Can't? Or Won't?"

"Can not."

I sighed. "Okay. I don't understand why."

"Duty."

Duty? What kind of an answer was that? "So, back home, wherever you are from, is there someone waiting for you?"

"Sister."

"Just her? No girlfriend? No wife?"

"I no cheat." His face tightened, which relaxed me. I may be an eventual notch on his bedpost, but at least he wasn't a cheater. "I has no one. At home."

"Me either, for what it's worth." None seemed

interested, and apparently, even a smooth-talking sweetheart like him couldn't get past my defenses either. I was hopeless and destined to be a little old lady all alone in my bar.

Antonio wrapped his arm around my waist and pulled me in close enough to feel his heart beating beneath my palm. A long finger pushed away part of my bangs and trailed down my cheek and over to my lips. It was like sweet little zaps of electricity, and it was wonderful and intoxicating. He cupped my chin, tilting it up and brushed his lips over mine.

I wanted more, and I sought it out, but he stepped out of reach.

"Show me more."

I swallowed at his unexpected comment. "Of me?" My voice cracked because I still wanted to but wasn't sure how. Yet.

He chuckled as he stared deep into my eyes. "Of Bay. Of your home."

"Oh, yes." I gathered my senses as the butterflies slammed into the wall. "Of course. Anything in particular? What would you like to see?"

"All."

Well then, I was going to be his tour guide, and I mentally tabulated a variety of sights. Cheshire Bay wasn't too big, and most of the interesting sights were within walking distance. It was the better way to see. We weren't just lighthouses and pubs. Our stores were delightful, although as

I glanced at the clock, most would be closing soon.

"Want to walk around the town? It isn't too big, and I can show you anything you want."

"Perfect."

I locked up my place and we headed down. "Would you like to see the wharf?" His brows knit together. "It's where the boats dock. There are a nice variety of sailing boats and the odd yacht or two."

"Show me."

We headed toward the dockside of our peninsula, all the while I filled him in about the school we passed, and how my graduating class was only twelve people. He laughed and mentioned his group was in the hundreds. There wasn't even a hundred in our school between kindergarten and grade twelve. To my running list of clues about Antonio, I added how he must've at least grown up in a metropolis of some sort to have had so many in one grade. Clearly it was not small town, population 1200.

The best part of our walk was the way Antonio took in every word I spoke. It thrilled me to have someone so interested in what unimportant information I spewed out.

We stopped at the rickety entrance to *Wharf Point*, a weathered white wooden beam with a sign, originally painted in the 70s, dangling from it. Although the sign hadn't changed, the docks had recently undergone an extensive upgrade and expansion, and I enjoyed grazing up and down the floating boardwalks checking out all the fancy boats.

"This is the wharf. A lot of people will dock here. Some even live in them full time and travel around the world."

I pointed to the boat buildings off to the far side, where a few were parked year-round. The buildings accounted for a third of the dock space. The rest were open docks and featured an array of motorboats, sail boats and the fancier, more expensive ocean cruisers – the yachts.

"Boating nice way to travel."

"You've travelled on one of these?"

Even under the glow of the streetlights, there was a tinge to his cheeks.

Yeah, he didn't just travel on one of those, my gut said he *owned* one of them. But which one? Was it the thirty-foot sailboat? The yacht with the darkened windows?

One by one, I pointed to the smallest boat, making a game out of it. Antonio shook his head, grinning as I attempted to hide the growing curiosity in my voice.

Walking down the docks, I'd nudge. "This one?"

"No."

And the game continued until we got into the bigger boats, the granddaddies of the meek sailors. The kind of boats you stared at as it pulled into the harbour. There were two of these grand vessels docked.

I took a chance and pointed to the smaller of the two. "That?"

"No. That one."

That one was at least a hundred feet long, and I suspected it had to back into the dock as it was pointed toward the opening of the inlet. It had two visible levels, all with darkened windows. The sleek exterior with red canvas deck chairs sent my imagination running wild with curiosity over what the inside was like, and the type of occupants it carried across the ocean.

"You've been on that?"

He nodded and there was a flicker of change behind his eyes. "Like mine."

"Like yours?" My jaw unhinged at the knowledge I'd been correct. Antonio wasn't just a developer; he was a mega-rich developer. "You own one of these?"

The guy was beyond loaded. Wow. It was crazy how I hadn't truly suspected as much all along. He did arrive with his own flight crew, after all.

"Grand Divertmento."

What? Oh, right. "That's what you named your boat? What does *divertmento* mean?"

"Big fun, bad name." He shook his head as he laughed.

Big fun? Yeah, it was funny, a horrible name mind you, but funny. Mind you, I could relate - my pub name wasn't much better – *Amber's Ale*. "Where do you cruise to?"

"Mediterranean Sea."

Jiminy Crickets. My geography knowledge was fairly

limited, but I knew where that was. Damn. What would it be like to sail on that sea?

"That's on my bucket list of places to visit when I'm old and retired."

"Better when young."

"Perhaps, but I'd need the money to get there. That'll come in about twenty years." Unless I struck it rich in a lottery I never played.

"May be," he broke it into two distinct words, "some day soon."

I laughed, and let the words fall out of my mouth, and cocked my head to the left. "You going to be the one to take me?"

"Why not? It be good."

I swallowed and tried to contain my stare. Surely, he was only saying it to be polite.

"Do you not like travel?"

"I'd love to, I don't have the means to travel. The furthest I've been to is the mainland, to Vancouver. Otherwise, I've been on this island all my life, even though I have a passport, which I need in case I travel to Seattle."

Eric sometimes flew over there, and every once in a while, I've wanted to catch a flight just to go and see what Seattle looks like. Some day I'll find it in me to actually buy a ticket.

"All your life?"

I nodded. I didn't want for much though. Everything I needed was tucked into this small section of the planet. "Where's the best place you've ever been?"

He rubbed his chin, and we started our walk toward the shore, as waves gently slapped against the dock. "Greece is beautiful."

"I can only imagine."

"Some day, I will show off." His fingers entwined with mine.

As much as I'd like to hold him to that, I knew it would never happen. Tonight was a one-off thing. There's no way the likes of him would purposely come back here, and there's no way the likes of me could ever afford to go where he was. We were like oil and vinegar; sure we were mixing, but it wouldn't take long for us to separate.

We stepped off the wooden docks and back onto the gravel paths. "Well, what else would you like to see?"

He lifted his shoulders high. "I do not know what is here."

Hmm. We were on the eastern edge of the peninsula. There wasn't much out this way aside from a lighthouse, and a tiny bridge which if we walked across, would put us close to the road leading him back his motel.

There was one other place. "Do you like dancing?"

"Ja."

"Then, let's check out *The Cowboy Den*."

It was a nice easy walk to the western pub.

"Like yours?"

"No." I laughed and didn't even try to contain myself. "There's no dance floor in mine. Just a cozy little place for people to socialize and unwind. We keep the music volume at a respectable level. It's peaceful."

In the heat of the summer months, the outdoor patio was a complete 180 to the inside. The music was much louder, but the clientele was different too. Younger and full of energy. They often had their own dance parties in the sand just off the gigantic porch.

"Peaceful good."

"Yes. It's the best way to unwind." Especially after a long day, and thankfully, this area was chalk full of places to relax. Not that we needed it really, the town itself was fairly laid back. It was a great draw for the tourists though, a nice change from their urban lives.

We walked in a comfortable silence down the road, the occasional car driving by.

Antonio squeezed my hand and faced me as we approached the road leading to the den. "You like being boss?"

"I don't mind it. The worst part is having to fire someone, but thankfully..." I ran to the nearest tree and rapped my knuckles against the trunk. "I've only had to do it twice. But yeah, for the most part, I like being in charge. I like the control."

"Me too."

"You're the boss? Of your real estate company?"

"Ja." He nodded, a sly smile inching out the left side. Damn it was cute.

"In… Italy?"

He chuckled at my weak attempt to discover more about him. "The boss of many."

"Of many? Like a hundred employees?"

He pointed up.

"A thousand?" The whites of my eyes grew.

"More."

Wow. I didn't need to know how many more. If he had that many employees, his hourly income was far superior to my yearly income. "No wonder you can travel so much. I have five, six including myself, on payroll."

"We all start small." He stopped and lifted my hand, planting a tender, toe-curling kiss on my hand. The tingling sensations firing away in my body were a pleasant surprise and I fought to breathe out normally.

"I suppose we do."

We stopped outside the busiest bar in town, a true country and western gem, complete with guys and gals donning traditional cowboy hats and boots, and huge, shiny belt buckles. It tickled me to see the scene because most of the islanders were laid back beach types, but with the people mingling out and about the main doors, you'd never know it.

The music blared when the old-fashioned saloon-styled door opened, and a patron stumbled out.

"Care to check it out?" I asked, curious to see if this was his jam. Somehow, I highly suspected he was more of a jazz music fan.

He tipped his head to the side. "Ja, sure."

A drunk cowboy staggered out the door as we were passing by. "Evenin' miss." His words were slurred, and his breath reeked of too much gin.

I tried my best to ignore him, but he grabbed my arm.

"I said, evenin'."

"You'd better let go of me." I bored into his eyes, determination tightening my muscles as I readied for action. He was taller than me and thick through the shoulders, but if he didn't let go, he was going to find himself in a world of pain.

Instead, the jerk laughed.

Before I had a chance to show this guy he messed with the wrong gal, Antonio grabbed the guy by the shirt collar.

Unfortunately, in my surprise reaction, I had not anticipated on Antonio pushing me out of the way, and I misstepped, slamming into the wall and cracking my head. As the guys roared, I slid down to the ground, covering myself.

Chapter Eight

I looked up and stared around Antonio, over to the cowboy who had his fists up, ready for a fight.

"Leave. Now." His voice commanded attention, as the murmuring ceased, and all eyes readied for a showdown. Antonio inched closer to me, putting distance between him and the cowjerk.

Apparently, cowjerk had an ounce of smarts as he skedaddled away.

Antonio bent down to help me up. "Let us get help."

I rubbed the back of my skull and blinked a few times to focus. It smarted, but there was no blood. "I'm okay. Stunned, but okay."

He shielded me from the crowd and pointed to a nearby lookout. "There." Arm wrapped tightly around my shoulders, he guided me over to one of the unoccupied benches. "Sit."

It was a good idea as my legs were quivering from the adrenaline my body was trying to burn off.

I really should've gotten into a better stance; it would've prevented me from making contact with the wall, but I'd been ready for the cowjerk's move, not Antonio's. I pulled my legs up under me and tucked my head onto my knees.

Antonio's hand rested between my shoulder blades. "You safe now."

Tears I didn't want to fall betrayed that request, and silently slipped down over my cheeks, although there was no reason for them. Nothing had happened, and nothing *likely* would've happened. Still, I kept my head hidden from Antonio, but no doubt, he felt the shaking in my chest since he pressed himself into me and wrapped me tighter in his arms. It only took a minute to gain control, but it was enough for the fault in my armour to have shown.

I needed a distraction. "Tell me about your family. Anything."

His chest rose and fell beneath my cheek, and his fingers rubbed my arm. "Mother and Father live Malta, in Mediterranean Sea. My sister, Maia, live in Naples."

Oh geez, he was Italian. My heart pounded at the thought of sitting beside a rich, handsome, and charming Italian.

"I born in Barcelona but live in Germany most of life."

"Wow. You're really a world traveller."

I stayed in his arms even though I desperately wanted to look up into his eyes.

"Ja. German was language one, Spanish two, Croatian three."

"Croatian?" Geography wasn't at the top of my favourite subjects, so I tried hard to picture where that was in relation to the others. I wasn't successful because I didn't think it was anywhere near the Mediterranean Sea. "How many languages do you speak?"

"Nine."

Nine? Wowsers. How unskilled was I? I knew English and a little bit of the local Haida language, but only what was common knowledge, and I only knew the written words. If someone spoke it to me, I was lost in translation.

"I learned English for girl."

I pushed out of the embrace and stared at him. "Oh yeah? A romantic, are you? Picked up a new language to impress a girl?" It was sweet.

"Emelia was to be wife."

Wife. The word echoed in my brain and even though he said he didn't cheat, words rolled off my tongue. "You are married?"

"No." Even though he continued to keep his arm around me, a far away expression shadowed his face. "Emelia died."

"Oh." My tone softened as his face pinched in pain. "You don't need to talk about it. It's okay. I'm sorry I brought it up."

As if I hadn't spoke, he carried on. "She died two years ago. Car crash."

I rubbed his cooled hand. "I'm sorry. That must've been hard to get over."

"It is."

I snuggled deep into him. "Can I ask you something?"

"Ja."

There were a million questions swirling in my head. "Never mind."

I didn't want to really know the answers anyway. It was only curiosity to things that weren't any of my business, and he'd soon be gone, never to come back to the likes of this tiny town.

Instead of talking, I listened to him breathe, slowly and rhythmically, like he didn't have a care in the world, something I envied.

He interrupted my thoughts with a question. "Want dance?"

My cheek rubbed against the soft material of his shirt. "No, thank you. I'd rather not go back in there."

"No, here. Under stars?"

I gazed into the sky. A million pinpricks of light danced overhead, and the rise of a full moon was just beginning. Dancing under the stars would be so romantic, corny, and only something that happened in the movies.

"Dance. With. Me." It was the first complete sentence he'd spoken, and the sweet grin on his face was so hard to resist. He rose and extended his hand.

I darted my gaze around, checking for some hidden cameras ready to announce how much of a fool I was for accepting his hand, but I saw nothing in the shadows of the tress.

"Okay." I timidly slipped my hand into his.

He snagged an arm around my waist, and we shifted back and forth to the slow beat rolling out of the bar. I rested my head against his chest, and for good measure I pinched myself on the arm just to prove I wasn't dreaming. I wasn't. I don't know how long we stayed locked together, but it was mesmerizing as it was just the two of us, shuffling our feet on the edge of a scenic outlook with the expanse of the Pacific Ocean steps away.

At one point, I pulled back to gaze up into his face and he stared down into my eyes. I stretched up on my tippy toes to kiss him, and his mouth claimed mine when I parted my lips and gave him permission. The kiss heated me up, and pleasure waves radiated out to my fingers, down to my toes, and settled into my core like never before. I could've kissed him all night, and it wouldn't have been enough. I wanted more. I needed more. And for the first time in a long while, I craved more.

"Let's go back to my place." I breathed out as his kisses trailed over my chin and to the nape of my neck. I gripped his hand, and pulled him past the bar, and past the entrance to the wharf.

Under the streetlight we stopped, where he kissed me again, the passion and fire burning brighter and more intensely than it had just ten minutes ago. My hand snaked under his jacket and touched his muscular back, releasing a groan from him and further fueling my desires.

Ten more fast paced minutes and we were at the stairs to my loft. The parking lot deserted as the clock ticked past midnight. I stood on the stairs, putting myself eye to eye with him. I leaned forward and held his face between my hands and kissed him hard. He responded with a deep, guttural moan.

"Let's go in," I panted.

Racing up the stairs, I kicked off my shoes and tossed my jacket to the couch, Antonio doing the same. Slowly, I led him down the hall to my bedroom where a more luxurious bed than the one at his motel greeted us, and I turned Antonio, gently pushing him onto it. I straddled his legs and seductively planted a teaser beside his lips and kissed across his whiskery cheek and over to his ear lobe, where I proceeded to flick it with the tip of my tongue before I popped it into my mouth and gently sucked it.

To my delight, he groaned and tightened his grip around my waist which spurred me on. I re-kissed the trail back to his mouth, the prickles of his whiskers tickling the nerve endings in my highly sensitive lips, and sending the energy into my heated core, which had turned from glowing embers into a full out fire.

He parted his lips, allowing me full control, and I kissed with all my heart, probing the depths of him, and feeling a heat and ache swell within me. My hands threaded through his incredibly soft hair, pulling him as close as possible. I yanked on his shirt, trying to free it.

In two quick moves, Antonio pulled the shirt free of his magnificent body, exposing me once again to a well-defined chest. He stared into my eyes as his hands settled upon my shoulders. Casually, I undid my shirt buttons, starting at the bottom and working my way up. When I reached the top, I opened and showed off my royal purple bra.

Goosebumps decorated my skin, but this time, they weren't from the cold. Tenderly, Antonio kept eye contact and caressed my shoulders as the material slipped further down to my hands, which I pulled free.

His hands returned to my pants and gently shimmied them over my hips, puddling them on the floor beside his shirt. "You are sexy."

In that moment, I was feeling it too. My skin was on fire, and my chest was heaving at the possibility of what we were doing. For a heartbeat, I blinked and held my breath as he traced a finger across my collarbone, my mouth falling open in delight. With the greatest of care, he slipped it under my bra strap and pulled it over my shoulder.

Reaching behind my back, I unhooked the purple ends, letting it fall down the length of my arms. Shielding myself, I ran my hands over his defined chest muscles and back up again, wrapping under his arms and exploring the rigidness of his back.

"You are incredibly handsome," I purred before I lowered my head to kiss him, to keep the flames burning, and he did not disappoint. The velvety softness greeted me and heated me up, despite how cold I was.

He stood, breaking our kiss, but in another quick move, his pants were on the floor and he stood there in his tight boxer briefs which left nothing to the imagination. The sight of him was incredible, and a thing of dreams.

"Wow…" There wasn't a right word for it.

He lowered and whispered, his breath tickling my ear and warming me at the same time. "I want you."

"I'm all yours." I swallowed and stared into his pools of blue, knowing he was going to be sweet, going to be patient, and above all, he was going to rock my world.

Like fine china, he hooked me under my knees and shoulders, carrying me to the bed, his eyes taking in my mostly naked body and filling with desire. I sat and touched his chest, which shook beneath my hand and glided my fingers down to his waistband.

A low groan grew in his throat. "Ember." My name had never sounded so sweet.

I hooked into his underwear and slowly pulled them down, the heat and ache in my core building the longer I took, but his skin was so firm and fine, I purposely took my time relishing the tightness beneath my sensitive fingertips. Desire spread across Antonio's face and it bulged out of him as the underwear lowered.

"Oh, God." He whispered as he hovered over me in all his naked glory. He lowered his head to claim my lips with a kiss that threatened to undo all my restraint as his hand threaded through mine and drew it over to his chest. His hand followed the length of mine, trailed across my neck, and stopped just above the swell of my chest.

I gave him a slow nod, and his finger moved further south, between my breasts and teasing across a nipple. I arched my back and pushed myself closer.

He lifted me to the edge of the bed and lowered himself onto the floor, placing his hands on my hips, fingers under the waistband.

From deep inside, a heavy moan poured out of me.

He kissed the inside of my quivering knees. "You okay?"

"I've just never..." I couldn't even say the words out loud, only having ever been kissed in one place before.

"Never?"

I shook my head and covered my chest.

"You enjoy." His eyes flashed and he expertly lifted my butt and pulled off my panties.

Slowly, he caressed the insides of my thighs, and each movement upwards, I opened a little more. And each time, he planted more kisses inside my knees. It drove me wild.

When his mouth made the trek to my core, I was ready to fall apart from the intense buildup, and it didn't take long for me to grab his head and scream out his name while my body shuddered from the most sensual feelings I'd ever felt. It was wave after wave of glorious heart-pounding sensations. Breathless, I begged him to be with me, to join me, to connect with me.

Antonio did not disappoint, and after rolling on a condom, he teased me with his tip, in and out, groaning as he went. Finally, he inched into me slowly, and I gasped at the size of him, breathing hard. Gently, he rocked in and out, each time the connection deeper until he was as deep as he could go. Together, we moved in time and he kissed me, a sweet scent and taste upon his lips. His hand covered a breast, giving it a little squeeze.

He dropped his hand suddenly and thrust once, twice, three times, calling out. "Ember."

"Yeah?" I closed my eyes and let the name swim in my head, as I drifted away in an ecstasy fueled fog.

"Ember. Look. At. Me."

I did.

"You. Okay?" There was a sheen of sweat on his forehead, but I focused on his eyes.

"Never better." I pulled him close and kissed him on the lips. I repeated it when we broke apart. I never believed sex truly had an element of love to it but I sure as hell felt it for the first time in my life.

"Thank you." I breathed out.

Chapter Nine

The illumination from my bedside table was enough to pierce the darkness when I blinked awake and rolled over.

Antonio stirred beside me, and I reminded myself it hadn't been a dream. It had been reality, one I never thought I'd have.

"Shh," I whispered and patted his strong chest. "Go back to sleep."

"You leave?"

At this hour, even a whisper seemed to echo off the walls.

"I'm going to go make coffee and take you out to meet a sunrise." I planted a kiss upon his whiskery cheek.

"Time?" He was fading in and out.

"It's 4:51 in the morning."

A half grin appeared on his face as he lifted his head off the pillow. "For sunrise?"

"It rises at 6:05, but I figure if we leave here in twenty minutes, we'll be able to catch the whole thing."

He grunted and rolled over, but reluctantly got out of my bed. How sweet was that? I actually had a man in my bed. It finally happened. Cedar would be so proud.

Cedar!

I grabbed my phone and scrolled through the messages. Her concern in where I'd been all night was fun to read, and I suspected all she did was stare at the various locations while Antonio and I walked all over town. The tracker stayed on my home as the last stop, but it was time to turn it off. Keep her in the dark, just a little. I'd explain it all to her later.

Coffees ready, I tossed on a sweater and a good pair of runners. Antonio had no qualms about doing the proverbial walk of shame and damn if he didn't look amazing in his expensive suit jacket and beige pants.

The best viewpoint to watch the sunrise was on southernmost tip of the peninsula, so we drove through the sleepy town and parked in front of his motel. From the parking lot, it was a leisurely walk.

"Did you need anything from your room?"

He shook his head, his blinks long. There hadn't been much sleep between us, an hour or two tops.

"Grab your coffee and let's go." I, too, should be way more tired than I was, but I was pretty sure I was jacked up on adrenaline and a little something else. The caffeine in the coffee would surely keep me jumping.

Dawn was brewing as the sky started to lighten. I jumped out of the truck and over to Antonio's side. Before another breath could escape my lungs, he bent down and tipped up my chin, planting a sweet, passionate-fueled kiss upon my lips. I melted on the spot as the heat grew and a warmth spread across my cheeks.

Darting my gaze around the desolate parking lot, unable to shake off a feeling of being watched, I turned to scan the motel. And my heart skipped a beat when I spotted her.

Sorcha. Leaning against the stairwell again. Didn't the woman sleep?

"C'mon." I tugged on Antonio's hand, and refocused on the reason for being here. Soon, she would have her claws back in him, but for now, he was mine. "Let's go watch the sunrise and you can give me your best visitor impression. Sunset versus sunrise."

"Lead the way." He was slowly waking up, as the gravelly sound was fading.

We walked hand in hand through the darkened forest. It was eerily silent as the only bird awake was a hooting owl in the distance. The air was damp and scented with a whiff of coffee whenever Antonio or I had a quick taste. The treetops heavy with dew thinned out to the light inky stain of sky, brightening with the oncoming sunrise.

"Do you want to walk out to the point?"

The lighthouse sent beams of light out across the fog-filled bay. If ever there was a morning to witness the birth of a new day, I was grateful Antonio would see this one. It all had the makings of a perfect, Cheshire Bay sunrise. One for the books.

"Ja, sure."

I swallowed down another gulp of coffee, although I'd never felt more awake nor more alive. Sharing something as personal as a sunrise was a new one for me even if it was with someone who was on his way out. Then again, the past few hours had been a series of new adventures.

The walk was easy going, a musical melody of waves crashing against the rocky escarpment, the air heavy with sea mist, and the far away cry of a gull out on the bay.

"Isn't it amazing?" My voice a bare whisper. To me, anything louder would shatter the beauty.

Antonio glanced around. "No sun?"

"It's coming. Just watch." I pointed to the east at the breach of the horizon with one hand and squeezed his hand with my other. My favourite way to start the day was beginning. "You'll see."

"I like what I look at." But he wasn't staring toward the dawn of morning, and he wasn't watching the lighthouse off in the walkable distance, he was looking right at me.

The words *but the sunrise* failed to come out of me as

he silenced all syllables with his coffee-tasting lips. The intensity of his sweet kiss grew from delicate to all out powerful, rendering thoughts of a sunrise null and void. It was beyond perfection.

Breaking apart breathless and wanting more, he stood beside me, and I rested my head against him, my free hand laying on his chest.

"Thank you." I threw the words out into the open ocean air.

"For me?"

"To whatever caused your plane to malfunction and have you land in my world. I never knew I could feel this."

He turned me to face him, a hint of fear in his eyes. "Feel?"

"Happy, so unbelievably happy."

A sadness washed over him, and he looked deeply into my eyes, a lone finger trailing down my cheek. "I go soon."

"I know." And knowing that, a tiny splinter streaked across my heart.

We walked back to the motel holding hands and were greeted by the Captain, as he descended the stairs in a full panic.

"Mr. Welsh, it is time to depart." He tapped his Rolex in rapid fashion.

Sorcha came up beside me, a smug smile on her face.

"Party time is over. Mr. Welsh has a meeting at nine. The clients have agreed to meet in Victoria, and it's imperative he attends."

My gaze flittered between the two men and over to Sorcha. Antonio had said it was cancelled, yet the Pilot was insistent it was going to happen. Wasn't Antonio the boss? Didn't he have final say?

Sorcha ignored me and spoke only to Antonio. "We have an inbound right now picking you up immediately. There it is." A satisfied grin pushed against the apples of her cheeks.

I glanced up the road to the black limo driving down the hill. Like a train wreck, I was unable to stop watching as it approached and parked in the empty lot.

"Monsieur Welsh?" The chauffeur opened the passenger door.

"Antonio?"

He strode up to me and touched my cheek with a sadness in his eyes. "I go. We knew this day ends."

I understood but I didn't want to let him go, too afraid to never see him again. That had been part of the deal – not to get too close, but somewhere through the night it happened, and my heart splintered at the thought.

"Time to go. Your plane is on final approach." Sorcha produced his suitcase and handed it to the chauffeur. She stood uncomfortably close to us.

How the hell did she have access to his room?

"Ember."

Tears formed as I tried to ignore her, and take in all of Antonio, but I had no response to his heartbreaking word.

He held my face and kissed me, but it was different; it was more emotional, fueled by pain and desire. "Bad bye."

"What?" I was sure I'd misheard.

"There no good about this."

"Mr. Welsh, please." The Captain urged him into the vehicle and climbed in after.

Sorcha stayed by my side and turned her back to the car. "Don't get too upset by this. He does this at every layover, makes every woman feel like she's his entire universe." She ran her gaze over me. "You're nothing special, just another notch on his belt. You should get tested."

In a move I didn't anticipate, she reached out and hugged me before stepping back to the car.

I blinked hard.

What the hell was that? Tested?

The chauffeur closed the door, tipped his hat, and drove them away. Just like that. No fanfare, nothing.

I covered my heart with one hand and stared as the wheels rolled over the gravel and back onto the road, questioning what Sorcha has said. It had to be a lie, either that or I was the most gullible woman in the world to believe what had happened between us was all an act. My instinct told me it was real, it had to be. I'd felt it to my very core.

How dare Sorcha plant a seed of doubt. Antonio was far too caring to have played me for a fool. He was the real deal. I knew it. I trusted my instincts, which over the years, have never failed. Tonight—this morning—the last eighteen hours, it had all been real.

If true love was like it was in the movies, he'd stop the limo and come back to sweep me off my feet and prove beyond a shadow of a doubt I wasn't another notch.

"Wait!" Like the world's biggest idiot, I ran after the limo, but it kept going, cresting the hill, and taking a sharp left.

I ran back down to my truck. I could see him off at the airport, it would be so romantic. My chance wasn't gone yet.

I put the pedal to the metal, but my old beater of a truck didn't stand a chance at catching the top-of-the-line limousine. And where had that come from? The nearest major city was at least two hours away.

I raced down main street, pulling hard onto the highway leading to the airport. How fast was the limo moving as I didn't see it on the road? Taking another hard turn, the tires squealed, and the engine groaned as I redlined it to the airport building, tucked just off the highway. My truck nearly hit the building when I slammed on the brakes, but the limo was nowhere to be seen.

Did I have the wrong airport? Were they going to drive across the island to Victoria? I hopped out of the truck and ran to the door, shaking the locked door on the building as hard as possible. No one was inside.

The building wasn't that long, so I ran the outside, turning at the corner. Part of the runway lay before me. I rounded the corner, and despair and a ragging heartache smacked me in the gut and slapped me across the face. There was no plane on the tarmac, and no limo parked nearby either.

No chance for a grand gesture at love, despite finally knowing I wanted it. Notch or not, I needed to know where I stood with him. If only I had a way to contact him. He was always on his phone, but I didn't know the name of his company, or even what city he worked in, but his number would be listed somewhere, and I knew just the person to obtain it for me.

Cedar.

She'd illegally tapped into a person's account to access personal information. She could do it again.

Chapter Ten

epeatedly I buzzed Cedar's apartment. Over and over again until she responded. But she didn't answer over the intercom.

Mitch opened the glass door at the entrance to the building. "What the hell, Amber?"

"Oh, please, you've got to help me."

"What's going on?" Cedar stood behind Mitch and pushed herself into my line of sight. "What's wrong?" Cedar let go of Mitch and wrapped her arm around me.

"He left. She said I didn't mean anything. But there were feelings. I know it. I need to get in contact with him. I need to know the truth. I need his number. I wasn't ready to say goodbye. Please, you need to help me."

Her warm hand touched my shoulder. "You're not making any sense. Come upstairs, and I'll get you some tea."

"I don't want any tea." It came out sharp and bitter. "I

need his contact information. And you can get it for me." I fell to my knees, and gave her my sweetest, plea filled request. "Please, you are the only one who can access the information in the computer."

Her eyes went large. "Are you asking me to break into confidential information."

"Yes, yes." I rose and pulled on her arms. "Please. I just need a number. Nine little numbers. Easy peasy."

"I can't do that. I'm on probation." She tugged me up to my feet. "What is this all about, and please calm down."

My focus jumped between her and Mitch, and over to the door, and back outside. "He left but we weren't ready."

"Who?"

"Antonio and his crew." I stared, begging her to remember.

She threw a glance to Mitch before focusing on me. "Amber, I'm so confused. Whose crew?"

"Antonio."

"I don't know who that is?" She shook her head.

My breath was catching in my chest and the words were getting harder to speak. I pleaded to her and Mitch. "You're. Wasting. Time. Please."

Cedar slapped me across the cheek and stepped back, her jaw dropping from her own actions. "Oh god, I'm so sorry. You were getting hysterical."

Mitch's eyes widened, but he didn't do a thing aside

from flip his gaze between his fiancée and me.

I held my hand against the angry mark, and after taking a much-needed deep breath, let my silent tears fall.

"What's going on? Tell me what happened. C'mon." She wrapped her fingers through mine and gently pulled me in the hallway, leading the way up the stairs to their floor and over to their apartment.

"Now sit. Mitch, get her some ice." My best friend sat beside me, her voice heavy with concern. "Who's Antonio?"

"The guy you sent over to see me yesterday."

"And he left?"

She was so calm, and her voice was so soothing, it took me a second to collect my bearings. "With his crew. The ones who flew in here. They said he had a meeting."

"Oh, okay. Things are becoming clearer. Now, just breathe."

I inhaled and took the small bag of ice Mitch offered me.

"Again, I'm really sorry for slapping you."

"No, it's okay. Forget about it." Inhaling another deep breath, I then exhaled in a slow steady count of three. "I probably would've done the same to you."

She nodded. "Fill me in on this guy because you said you loved him?"

I wrapped my arms around my chest, the impossibility of having fallen for someone who was a complete stranger less than 24 hours ago. "We hit it off, Mr. Welsh and me. I mean, not at first, but after I drove him to the motel, we just sort of clicked. We had a nice dinner, went for a walk to watch the sunset and splashed in the bay." I skipped over our first sexual encounter. "After that, we walked around town and danced under the stars. We talked, he understood me. The first guy ever to just get me. This morning we watched the sunrise, having not slept all night."

It had all been so perfect. Too perfect, maybe. Like those too good to be true kind of moments.

My tone soured, as an image of Sorcha popped into my head. "Suddenly, his crew have his luggage and are pushing him to go, how he has a meeting. And the co-pilot, she said I was just another notch in his belt and that I should get tested." My shoulders rolled in and my focus went blurry. "Somehow, over the night, I fell for him, and I don't believe Sorcha, but I can ask him if you can get me his number."

I wasn't ready to let the best night of my life end so abruptly. I wanted more. I wanted Antonio.

"Oh, Am." She wrapped me in a hug, a sympathetic smile blossoming on her face. "You had the night."

"The night?"

"Everyone gets that one special night where they stay up all night long. It only happens with your soulmate."

I burst into tears. "And he's gone, see what I mean?"

"I'm so sorry. You were supposed to have a good time,

not fall for the guy."

"Can I get you anything to drink?" Mitch asked from the safety of his kitchen.

Wild women weren't his forte, and I still hadn't forgiven him for the temporary wedge he put between him and Cedar, even if they did work through it. Mitch had cheated on her, albeit shortly after they started going out, years ago.

I blinked and stared at them both, and at the clock hanging in their living room. "Oh, damn. You're supposed to be going to work." Cedar was dressed in her work uniform. "I'm so sorry." I rose and headed to the door. "Can you do me a favour, though? When you get to work, can you see where the plane left from? I went to the airport and there was no plane or limo for that matter. He just vanished. There must be a log of it somewhere, right? He left for Victoria."

"I'll see what I can do, and I can check with the tower." Cedar nodded and looked over at Mitch. "Why don't we drive you home and let you get some rest?"

I nodded. Sleep would be a good idea, but I needed to do some searching first.

"I'll take your keys, Amber." Mitch stayed a respectable distance but extended his hand.

I tossed him the keys and followed them out.

After they dropped me and my truck off, I curled up with my

computer and searched the internet. I had to know. If I was a notch, then there would be dozens of pictures with him and some form of arm candy at every event under the sun, right?

I typed in his name.

Antonio Welsh. A dozen hits about a basketball player.

Mr. Antonio Welsh. More basketball, a few other sites leading to information on some governor out of the states.

Mr. Welsh. A million results but nothing that came to anything remotely similar, and an image search showed no one familiar.

My brain was foggy and figured I needed a location to go with the name. I typed in *Antonio Welsh Italy.* Yeah, that was a mistake. Nothing of relevance.

What was his sister's name? Maybe that would help? And where was she from again? Not expecting anything, I typed in *Maia Welsh Naples.* The top ten results were interesting as most of them highlighted a Maya WELCH.

Hmmm. I rubbed my aching temples.

What about? Antonio Welch?

What if with the crew's weak accents, and the way Antonio struggled to pronounce any hard 'c', it just came out sounding like Welsh? I hit the return button and a whole new listing of sites appeared, and these were more interesting with business names attached to the hits, and not just about the basketball star.

I scrolled through pages of images, finally spotting

something that bore a resemblance. I clicked, and there he was.

At a ball in Cyprus, with a gorgeous redhead tucked in beside him.

On his boat with a rail-thin blonde in the tiniest bikini, as caught by some paparazzi and sold to the highest bidder.

Another in front of a fancy car, with yet another gal.

In front of a private jet, another redhead in a tight black dress hanging on his arm.

It *had* been an act. The whole damn thing. I wasn't anything special. I had been played.

One night or not, I'd let emotions get tangled into the mess, and fell for the dream that a foreign hottie would find me worthy of wanting to be with me for more than a quick overnight.

Antonio had acted so kind and caring, and I ingested all his smooth-talk, handsomeness, and even had sex with him. I'd let him into me, and into my heart, and it was all for sport.

I was so messed up, somewhere along the way, I'd hoped it wasn't a fantasy, but my mind played tricks on me. All along I'd spent the day with a billionaire jerk, who only confirmed that rich or poor, all men were the same – assholes not to be trusted.

I hated myself for feeling what I felt. For caving to the ideal which wasn't real. I'd been a way for him to pass time.

Reliving those magnificent hours shattered my heart. I closed my computer and grabbed a throw pillow to wrap my arms around as I cried myself to sleep.

I woke up in the mid-afternoon and begrudgingly readied for my evening shift. My phone had been silent – no word from Cedar, which likely meant she hadn't found anything worth reporting.

I headed down to the pub and glanced around, hoping against hope to see him. Of course, he wasn't there. He wasn't coming back. Ever. He was likely already onto his next conquest.

"Wow, you look beat, Amber. Why don't you take the evening off?" One of my shift managers stopped pouring a whiskey sour to study me.

"I'm fine. Honestly. I just have a lot on my mind, and I feel it would be better for me to be here." Plus, I had inventory in the back room to count and scheduling to arrange around the upcoming Thanksgiving weekend and throughout the rest of the month. "I'll be in the office if you need me."

I plunked down in my chair and pulled out the staffing requests, going by who wanted what day off for the long weekend. It didn't take long though, and the schedule was done. It probably helped I was closing the store for the actual holiday. I wished everything in life was as simple as that.

With a quick print out, I hung the new shift schedule on the staffing board and went into the back room with my iPad. Inventory wasn't a whole lot of fun, but it was menial and required I concentrate on the task at hand. Something I desperately needed right now.

However, when I touched a bottle of wine, I was instantly transported to dinner last night and the smooth way Antonio ordered the wine and tasted it first. He knew then I could be played, and he prepped me with wine to weaken my defenses. Damn him. But the wine was surprisingly tasty – one I needed to add to my order list.

I counted out the rest of the wine bottles, imagining them as women in Antonio's life. How many others had there been before me? Did he have some kind of disease? Is that why Sorcha said I should be tested? If I didn't want word to spread through this town like fire, I'd need to see a doctor in another town. I flipped over to my calendar and set a reminder to look up clinics, preferably in Port Alberni.

Back to the counting.

When I got to the Jack Daniels, my first impression of Antonio flew to the forefront of my mind. He came across as arrogant and super serious, a total jerk. I should've kept my distance and listened to what my brain was saying. I shouldn't have offered to drive him to his motel. That had been my undoing, and that's when he probably figured out the way to weasel into my heart. Had I just let the rich billionaire find his own way, I wouldn't be stuck in the back room holding a bottle, with tears falling out in rapid fashion. Nope, had I just left him alone, I wouldn't have fallen for the handsome stranger.

A knuckle rapped on the door.

"Miss Amber? A guest up front is asking for you."

My heart skipped a beat. Was it him? Did he come back?

"Thank you, Dale." My back was to him so thankfully he didn't see the tears I was wiping away. "I'll be right there."

Confident he was gone, I dashed to the staff backroom and checked myself out in the mirror. Yeah, I looked rough, but whatever. I pinched some colour into my cheeks and with a spring in my steps, headed into the pub, scanning for him.

A hand near the back shot up and waved. It wasn't Antonio, because this was real life, and my heart dropped into the pit of my stomach.

I walked over and sat down with my best friend. "Hey."

"Geez, did you manage any sleep?" Cedar rubbed my back.

"A little, but I tossed and turned." I fiddled with one of the disposable coasters. "Did you find out anything?"

She sighed, a tell that the incoming news wasn't what I wanted to hear. "I talked to the guys up in the tower and they had nothing. So… I did a little digging."

My eyes lit up and a shiver of hope wiggled through my body.

"Nothing illegal," she warned, "but I called over to ATC to simply inquire if there was a flight that had left our region around the time you came over."

"Yeah?"

"There was an outbound helicopter flight from Port Alberni to Victoria, but other than that, he was tight lipped. I'm sorry."

"Would he leave via helicopter?"

"I honestly don't know. Their airport is smaller than ours, they only use helicopters and float planes. No runway, just a helipad. I don't think that was your guy."

My head fell onto my arms, and I stared at the floor. More lies. Probably wasn't on a plane at all. Had the fancy limousine to drive him all the way back to Victoria, to some gargantuan board room where he'd make the big real estate deal and then move on with his rich, fancy, Amber-free life.

"I'm sorry, Am."

I sat up, shaking away the utter disbelief. "I'm such a bloody idiot. I can't believe how stupid I was and how easily he played me. He'd only been the first guy to make me feel comfortable and desired, so of course, he's a jerk. Sorcha was right. I found pictures of him on the internet – different girl every time." I hated myself so much, it was turning my stomach. "You know, last night we tried to do the deed."

Not surprising, Cedar's eyes doubled in size.

"But I couldn't do it. Too much hesitation. And you know what, he was okay with that. Can you imagine?"

"That's huge." Because she knew about my track record with the male species, not the finer details mind you, but just enough to understand I didn't give it away to just anyone.

"It was all an act. Proved he was a good guy by not forcing himself on me. Bam. One point for the jerk – show her sex wasn't important, because he liked who I was in here." I stabbed my chest. "Make her want it more, right? It's like the universe keeps giving me a giant finger, only now I finally see it."

A sad smile teased her lips. "You got played, Am, and I'm so deeply sorry I sent him to you. That wasn't my intention." She bowed her head so we were forehead to forehead.

I sighed and straightened out, rolling my shoulders back now that my little rant was over. "Maybe it's time for me to rethink my deal here. Maybe I need to stretch out my wings and explore."

"I think you need to rethink that idea. Get a solid night of sleep first before committing to changing your whole life. You're seriously sleep-deprived and you're hurting. Don't do something you'll end up regretting."

"Too late," I said sarcastically as I grabbed her empty

113

Coke. "But I see your point. I'll get you a refill."

"Don't do anything foolish." She cupped her hands around her mouth and yelled it in my direction.

"Says the girl who sent a VIP over to ask for me by name."

My anger was misplaced. It shouldn't have been directed at Cedar, but Antonio wasn't around for me to take it out on him.

Chapter Eleven

I backed the truck up to the side entrance of the pub, the door nearest the storeroom.

Dale met me outside. "I've everything ready for ya."

"Thanks." I popped the end gate. "We'll load it up in there."

The big Thanksgiving bonfire was tonight, the last major one of the season. The weather was promising a great night, minimal clouds, and hardly any breeze. It couldn't have been more perfect weather wise if we'd begged and danced to the weather Gods, something Cedar joked she was more than ready to do.

At last count, late last night, there were over fifty people in attendance.

I lifted flat after flat of beer into the box. "You think this will be enough?"

Over the past three days, Dale had helped me decide

what alcohol to bring. It was a potluck of sorts; everyone chipped in money which went to booze and food. Naturally, I was in charge of the beers and bevvies.

"Ya, and if not, give me a holler. I can bring some over."

"You're welcome to attend without being my delivery guy, you know."

"That's awfully kinda ya, and I'll consider it."

Dale had been a friendly shoulder to lean on especially after he caught me having an outburst in the back room over Antonio. Busted, I'd then spilled how the charming SOB played me and asked him why all guys were jerks. Understandably, he said they weren't all like that. Knowing I'd offended him, it dug the knife in a little deeper, because he was right – it wasn't *all* guys, just the ones I seemed to associate with. Dale probably thought I was a tad crazy for having more emotions over the little bit of time I'd spent with Antonio than there was right to have, but still, he tolerated it, and me, just the same.

"Did ya call him?"

No, I hadn't. I'd tracked down one of the businesses he ran and had a nastygram ready to fire out to their general email department, but I never hit send. I had to learn it was one night and to let it go. It had been four days already. Besides, if it was real, he would've tried to get in contact, since he knew where I worked and lived. It wouldn't be hard at all to get in touch with me.

Dale grabbed another flat and handed it to me, where I added it on to the small stack I had going. "His mistake."

I shrugged. That was what Cedar and Mitch had said, and Eric too, who, incidentally, tried his best to get more information as well, and it was all for naught. Their empty plane had sat beside the building for less than twenty-fours when a new crew came in, repaired it *priority one,* and filed a flight plan to Victoria. There was no passenger manifest for the belly crashed flight.

"That's kind of you to say." I positioned the last of the flats. "That should do it." I hopped out of the bed and slammed the end gate.

Dale picked up a scrap of paper from the ground. "Can I ask ya somethun?"

"Of course."

"Being that this guy is history, would ya ever think about seeing someone else?" He looked at the ground and brushed his hands down his jeans. "Like say, me?"

Well, that was not quite the question I expected, and I didn't know how to let the guy down without hurting his feelings. Dale was nice, but I wasn't attracted to him, and even if I was, I wasn't ready to move on.

"I know I'm not super educated or anything, but I got me a good paying job at a great local establishment, and I've no warrants out for ma arrest or anything." A small wink came my way, but I wasn't sure if it was intentional since he rubbed his eye after talking.

"You're a great guy, Dale, and a fantastic employee." And that was my in. "But..." I leaned in and whispered. "I can't date staff. It looks bad, like I'm playing favourites." I leaked out a half smile.

"Ah, ya, that makes sense." He tapped his temple. "Don't tell no one I asked ya out."

I patted him on the arm. "I promise your secret is safe with me."

"We good?"

"We're all good. I think I have enough alcohol to keep everyone well hydrated." I looked inside the box and did another quick count on the flats in the box. "Yeah, should be enough. Thanks for your help." I opened the door of my truck and stood on the running board. "Offer still stands if you want to come for the bonfire tonight."

"Next time."

# # #

The bonfire was in full swing and people were celebrating all they had to be thankful for. I had to admit, despite all that life had thrown at me, I was pretty lucky, and had plenty to be grateful for.

I owned my own successful business and had a roof

over my head.

I had great friends, the best in the world, who loved me with all their hearts and were willing to slap some sense into me when I needed it most.

And aside from having someone I trusted with my heart, I had everything else I needed in life.

I stood on the edge of the beach, arm in arm with Cedar, my tummy full from the platefuls of food I'd consumed. Turkey, salads, mashed potatoes, homemade dessert, the works. If I ate before Christmas, it would be too soon.

"Great party, isn't it?" Her belly seemed a little bigger than normal. Guess the baby enjoyed Thanksgiving dinner too.

I rested my head against hers. "It really is. No one is severely intoxicated even though we somehow went through all the beer. Guess I misjudged that."

Which was odd because I'd triple checked the numbers.

"No one's touching the hard stuff, so that's probably why. Also, Riley said there were additional people. Something like ten others."

"That's why I didn't recognize them."

I tended to hang out with those I knew, as I was more comfortable with Eric, Cedar and Mitch – my relatively tight group. I was learning to like Lily the more I got to truly know her – she and I didn't hang out as teens when she was one of the summer brats visiting for the summer as I was at odds with her personality, but she'd come a long way since then and seemed to be a good fit for Eric. And *that* made me like her more.

"Willow and Arlo's kids came, which I guess was a last-minute decision."

Well, that would add to the numbers since they had three grown children who were each married.

"Oh, yeah, and Trent and Delilah came. Trent works in the tower and was alone for Thanksgiving." She faced me with seriousness on her face and a finger in the air. "Don't even think to ask him anything about the flight." She paused and softened her features. "Eric already has."

There went that idea.

"I appreciate the effort but I'm trying not to think about him." Even though he popped up in my dreams nightly.

"Why aren't you joining in more of the festivities? Come on over. Arlo's got the guitar and he's playing a haunting rendition of a Chris Isaak song."

"Oh yeah, which song?"

"Wicked something or other."

"Wicked Game?"

She perked up. "Yeah, that one."

That song. It was one of the songs playing in the distance the night Antonio and I danced under the stars; the speakers of the Cowboy Den sent it straight out to us.

"Thanks, but I'm waiting for an order from Dale. I requested a couple more flats. As the barkeep of this party, I need to fulfill my end." I winked.

"Always the bartender, never the drinker."

"Says you who has no drink in hand." I let my gaze drop to her tummy. "Of which I'm happy to see."

"Once Dale gets here, you'll come join us?" There was so much pleading in her features it was hard to turn her down.

"Maybe. Not sure if I'm in a sing-along mood."

"There's a group going skinny-dipping at the cliffs."

I gave her my best *not-going-to-happen* look. It wasn't my thing, Cedar's for sure, and I expected her to partake in that.

"Chicken." She skipped off over to the bonfire bathing the beach in an ocean of oranges and yellows, with dark shadows.

My phone pinged. Dale had arrived. Finally. Needed to give the guy explicit directions. Turn left here, turn right at the rock, sheesh. He was a great short order cook, but lousy with directions.

I walked between Eric and Lily's houses, onto the grass and out to where the vehicles filled the driveways and road. Thankfully, they were at the end of the road, so there was ample room to park.

Dale jumped out of his jeep and popped the hatch.

With a quick flick, he opened the end gate.

"Thanks for bringing all this. I appreciate it." I reached into the back as the front passenger side door closed.

"Can I be of assistance?"

No-freaking-way.

Chapter Twelve

That accented voice had haunted my dreams over the past few nights.

"Antonio?" But I already knew as I couldn't take my eyes off him. He was too sexy in his tailored suit, with the top button of his dress shirt undone – a GQ model for the well-dressed man issue.

"Ember."

Damn, my name still sounded so sweet rolling off his lips. Before his true intentions were revealed, I'd entertained a thought or two of changing it to that, but I rather liked how he was the only one to swap the *Ah* for the *Eh* so I decided against it. But that was then, this was now. He'd broken my heart with his abrupt departure, but more so from his lack of communication since. Even though we both knew he was leaving, and he'd only be here for one night, it was the way the whole situation unfolded like an explosion that left me reeling.

All the anger I had managed to tamper down, came roaring back to life.

I flipped my narrowed gaze quickly over to Dale.

He shrugged. "He came inta the pub asking for ya, after ya called. When he said who he was, well, I just knew he hadda come."

I glared and all the hurt and rage inside me built to epic levels of madness and shot out at Antonio. "You're a jerk."

Yep, that was the best I could throw at him. I dropped my flat down and yanked another, adding it on top and debated adding a third. Anger-fueled adrenaline made me super strong. A tad crazy, but freakishly strong.

Dale lifted them all from my hands. "I deliver. Ya talk."

"I have nothing to say. I waited for some form of contact, and it was radio silence. Yeah, I'm so done."

I grabbed another two cases and stacked one on top of the other and wrenched my back by twisting so violently away.

"Ember?" His voice was soft and genuine.

"God damn it. Why now? Why come back?" I dropped my head and took a breath.

This wasn't the time or place. Hands in a death grip around the beer boxes, I stormed between the houses and onto the beach, wrapping back to Eric's back porch.

We stacked them there where Eric was dumping in bags of ice to a couple of coolers. His head perked up as I climbed the stairs and set the cases down. "Great. This really should do…" He stopped and stared, so I spun around.

Antonio was right behind me carrying the final two cases.

"You have a lot of nerve showing up here, buddy." Eric's narrowed gaze shot daggers towards Antonio. "Who do you think you are?"

"I guy who came long way for bun-fire." His voice had an icy edge.

Eric stormed closer, and I immediately thrust up my hand and pushed against his shoulder, speaking in the calmest, but most collected voice I could conjure. "I will handle this."

Arm fully extended, but not locked, I shook my head, trying to ignore the sexy, jerk of a man whose exotic cologne ticked my nose with its spicy scent. Instead, I lavished attention on Dale.

"Eric, have you met Dale, my short order cook? He was gracious enough to bring over some more drinks." I patted Dale's arm for effect, which was probably a low blow as I worried Dale would misinterpret it and think I was sending out some truly mixed signals. I was the worst person in the world. No wonder karma bit me in the ass so hard.

The tension in the air between the four of us was thick as mud.

Eric shook Dale's hand but failed to remove his glare from Antonio. "Dale, grab a beer and join the party. Food is next door, nicely spread out on the back porch, and there's lots of it, so don't be shy." He flipped his gaze between Antonio and me. "You need my help to handle this?"

"No." It was terse and full of spite.

There was so much anger flowing through my veins, all directed at me because I'd allowed myself to have feelings when I damn well knew better. However, I wanted to hear the man out.

"I'll be right next door grabbing another plate if you need anything." But he didn't move, rather, Eric hung on the porch, leaning against the railing.

Out of the shadows, Mitch and Jesse approached.

"I've got this." It was meant for all the men currently staring, and as unnerving as it was, in many ways it was a small comfort knowing my surrogate family was ready to protect me.

However, I wasn't going to let the wolves circle any longer, and I motioned for Antonio to follow me away from the gathered testosterone, over to someplace with a modicum of privacy. Whatever we needed to discuss, this was between us.

He kept his distance respectable, staying a few feet behind.

I stopped at a part of the beach where the air was

crisper since we were further away from the bonfire, but we were safely out of earshot. The overhanging moon cast shadows of us on the sand, illuminating a log to sit on.

"Ember?" His voice was soft and pleading for me to face him, but I kept my back to him. "Why you angry?"

"Because I'm confused." I dug the toe of my shoe into the sand, burying it deep.

Antonio stepped around me. "I do not understand."

Did I start with how he just abruptly left and failed to find a way to contact me? Or did I mention the feelings that suddenly and overwhelming bloomed in me, and how I'd never felt like that with another guy, even though it had been less than twenty-four hours, and how utterly ridiculous it was to feel those emotions so quickly?

I went with the latter. "I told myself over and over how you meant nothing as you were just a guest here and how whatever happened – not that I expected anything to happen – it was just going to be a one-night thing. But sometime between giving you a lift in the truck and the sun rising, something changed."

He tipped my chin and looked deep into my eyes. "What changed?"

I twisted out of his touch, and for a moment my focus sprang to the deck where the three guys stood.

"It doesn't matter." I shook my head.

They were only feelings, stupid girly, over-reacting

feelings. I had tried to convince myself it had only been a dream, but over the past few days, I couldn't get the final images out of my head. As much as I enjoyed splashing in the bay, and kissing him, and having sex with him, those last images were of her contorted face and venomous words.

"Was I just another notch for you? Sorcha said so. Said you did this at every layover."

"Did what?" That sexy accent got under my skin like an itch I couldn't scratch.

My breath hitched and as I sat on the log, my voice fell to a near whisper. Only the rolling waves were louder. "Made someone fall for you."

A smile inched along the edges of his lips, and even with his face in a soft shadow, it was easy to see. "You fell for me?"

I jumped off the log when he reached out for me. "How could I not? You're a smooth business guy. Wasn't that your plan? Wine, dine and be everything I thought I needed, and then close the sale and disappear without a word."

"No. Not all. You were…" He circled his hand through the air. "What the word is?"

As I waited for him to spit it out, I added my own descriptors, because they were so close to the surface in how I felt. "Pathetic? Weak? Easily gullible?"

He narrowed his eyes and placed his hand on my shoulder. "No. You amazing lady."

"Save it, pal." I pushed his strong hand away. "I fell for your charm once, but I'm not doing it again. I can't. It wasn't real." I stepped away only to feel his hand wrap around my wrist. My instinct was strike out, but I reigned it in. "Let go of me." My strongest, bar-crowd breaking voice rolled out of me.

He dropped my hand like it was on fire, and I stormed away. "Please, Ember, hear me. I go long way to be here."

I double stepped and stopped. It was true. He was here, and he didn't live anywhere near the island, hell, he didn't even live on this side of the world.

Slowly, I turned around, emotions swirling in my gut, bubbles of anger popping in the boil.

"God damn it, Antonio." My foot slammed into the beach. "I live in the real world, and I know that this whole thing, and all these feelings, it's all on me but it wasn't real, even if it felt like it." My voice pitched. "It's my fault for believing in the magic of…"

I tossed my hands out to the side and paused. Had it been a smidgen of what falling in love was like? I didn't know.

"I let my emotions control me and allowed myself to fall for you and let you into a part of me I try very hard to keep sealed off to the rest of the world." Tears blurred my view as I covered my aching heart. If this is what a breaking heart felt like, I never wanted to experience it ever again. "So, thank you for coming all the way back here just to tell me I'm amazing."

I rolled my eyes. "I appreciate you taking the effort."

With that, I turned away so the tears could fall without him seeing. My focus went to the guys waiting for me, and I headed toward them.

"Ember." His voice was strong as it punctuated the air, silencing the general hum around me. "I not finished."

I stopped cold in my tracks but refused to turn around.

His fancy shoes dug into the sand as he approached. "How could I not be with you?" Gently, he placed his hand upon my shoulder and spoke with a softness to slice through my pain. "Please turn and look at me."

Keeping my head down, I did as he asked, staring only at his dress pants.

"I need more Ember. One night not enough."

How did he manage to say the things he did and melt my heart?

"Ha." Still, I wasn't going to give him an inch, and I crossed my arms over my chest after wiping my hand over my face. "I don't believe a word you're saying."

He tipped his head. "Why not?"

"Because I've seen the pictures, you with a different girl on your arm. It's all over the internet. Plus, Sorcha said I was just a notch in your belt."

"What mean that?"

I stepped closer. Even though we were out of earshot, no one needed to know I'd slept with a guy within hours of meeting him, although they probably all knew anyway. Small towns and all that.

"I was just someone to have sex with." I made a circle with one hand and poked a finger though. Wasn't that the international sign?

"Oh, no, Ember. You more. In here." His strong hands covered his heart.

I sent a spray of sand flying, wanting to believe his words. "I'm sure you say that to all the girls. I've seen the pictures."

A deep furrow formed between his brows. "Pictures? Ladies? Only ever have picture with four, and I know. I agree. Maia, Emelia, Genevieve…" He counted on his left hand.

Maia was his sister. Emelia was the fiancée. "Who's Genevieve?"

"Emelia's sister. Head of regional department of charity protecting battered ladies." He inched his way closer.

"Well, that's an honourable position." It was great he kept in touch with his former fiancée's family, but still, it didn't explain the other. "What about the redhead?"

"Sorcha?" It came out like a weak laugh.

Of course, like a mental smack to the head I saw it. She looked different when she wasn't in a flight uniform with her hair braided.

"Sorcha was girlfriend, now just friend. She is - how you say? Jealous? Especially now."

I listened and flipped over everything he said. The nasty way she glared at me when we connected at the motel, the cruel way she whispered her words. Yeah, jealousy described her well.

"You weren't just using me?" Because I still didn't believe him.

"Ja, but only to fill ache in heart." He placed his hands on my shoulders, so we were face to face. "You made me feel good. Alive. I happy with you."

"And I was happy too."

He stepped close enough to brush a strand of hair off my face. "That why I fly around world to see you."

All my life I'd wanted someone to pine after me and make me feel important enough to be with. Hearing Antonio say it and follow it with actions, my heart went into overdrive and my brain turned to mush – the rest of my thoughts vacated their logical resting place.

"You think I crazy?" His chin tucked into his chest. "Maia says no, says is something more. Something I not have since Emelia."

I reached for his hand and wrapped my own through it. "Maybe a tad crazy, since we only met by happenstance, and we live in two different worlds. Two. Very. Different. Worlds." Regardless, my heart swelled, and a sensation of butterflies took flight. "But it's not completely crazy either. When I was with you, I was totally happy. You make me feel things I haven't felt before."

He waited, but the smug smile on his face said it all. He just wanted to hear it. "Feel?"

"Strong feelings. Powerful feelings, but all good."

"Oh, Ember." He cupped my cheeks and brushed his lips across them. "I sorry I made you mad."

"Never make me sad again."

"I will promise." He bent down, but before I allowed those sweet lips to touch mine, I had something else on my mind.

I pushed his shoulder gently. "I need an explanation first."

His gaze locked with mine. "Anything."

"Why were the Captain and Sorcha in such a hurry to leave that morning? What was with the sudden urgency, and where the hell did you go? I went to the airport and you weren't there. I checked with the helipad in Port Alberni, and you never left from there either."

"Is long story."

"I have time." Let my friends pace on the deck a little longer.

He sighed and motioned to come and sit beside him on the log. "I had problem."

I sat and dug my feet into the sand, turning to give him my full attention.

"Forgive my bad English while explain." He sighed

and there was a long pause. "After plane accident, CEO was to lead at meeting. I cannot say about what." It was okay to not know the details on that, as it was something I understood. "He call many times over night."

"That's who that was." I nodded my understanding. Whatever deal was going on, clearly it was a big one.

"I sorry for interruptions."

"It's okay. Trust me, I understand business."

"Ja, thank you." He shifted. "In morning, I ignore CEO message by mistake. He had 'mergency with daughter and sent meeting to me from Seattle but only early hour work, not late afternoon."

"In Victoria?" It was starting to make a little sense. If the time got changed, and he wasn't expecting it, yes, it could explain most of it.

"Ja."

However, it was only part of the answer. "But after that, you never called me, or even tried to get in touch. You knew where I worked and lived, it would've been easy to get a hold of me."

"I did." His brows knit tightly together.

I tipped my head. "When?"

"Guy took call. Left number."

My jaw unhinged and I gaze around the rolling ocean. "You what? When?"

Where had that message gone? Someone at work had

a ton of explaining to do because all this time, I'd been hoping he had tried.

I shook my head, as a dull ache settled over my chest. "I'm sorry, I never got that message."

"That why I come to see you, Ember." He reached for my hand. "I could not leave you without answers. You here." His free hand pointed to his heart. "I need you." With a gentle pull up with the pad of his finger, he once again slowly pressed his lips to mine, this time with power, with desire, and with a feeling it was real. "I want you."

I gazed into his eyes reflecting the bright sphere of the full moon, a smile thinning my lips. "I want you too."

Threading my fingers through his soft hair, I pulled him close, breathing him in. From the tips of my fingers to the depth of my soul, I needed the connection with Antonio, and he did not disappoint. As he brushed his lips over mine, a longing and desire surfaced in me, and I allowed myself to fall.

It was the greatest feeling in the world, as the waves lapped against the shore and the moon illuminated the pair of us as we kissed on the beach. Dreams couldn't hold a candle to the reality.

I leaned my head against him as he wrapped his arms around and held me close. My senses told me we were being watched so I scanned the shadows until I saw them, over by Lily's deck. Eric, Lily, Jesse, Mitch, and Cedar all stood on the stairs.

A gentle heat crawled over my chest and face. "Well, Antonio. Now that we've cleared the air, there are a few people you need to properly meet."

"Ah, yes, your family."

We rose, walking away from the log and rolling surf. He stopped me mid-step and planted another, knee-weakening kiss upon my lips.

As much as I wanted to continue to melt into his arms, I sensed Cedar was ready to jump off the deck. It was time to join the group and introduce the man of my dreams.

Hand in hand, I walked him over to meet my buddies and to give me even more reason to be thankful.

Epilogue

Fourteen months later

I wiggled beneath the satiny sheets in his luxurious bedroom, in the bow of his yacht, a far cry from the standard rooms I'd travelled in the before times – the times before meeting and falling in love with Antonio. Brushing the flattened curls off my heated face, I rolled over to gaze into his handsome face.

"That's a helluva way to wake up." It was hard to wipe the perma-grin away.

"Ja, indeed." He kissed the tip of my nose.

We were south of Cheshire Bay, somewhere near the Oregon coast, enjoying a romantic week-long vacation, the third one in the past year. Outside on the expansive dock, the sun was nice, but the air was a bit cooler, and we preferred our private time in the bow, even though the three-man crew were like ghosts – I rarely saw them.

Having grown up on the poorer side of life, the wealth and expense of the places Antonio flew me to always took me by surprise. I felt like royalty, and at every destination, I've been treated that way too. It's surreal, but the break was nice, even if I missed my seaside village with all its small-town charm.

My phone pinged on the nightstand, and I stretched over my loving man to reach it, the weight of the new rock on my finger dropping my hand quickly to the table. Scanning the messages, I quickly typed back a response and set the phone back down.

"Everything all good?"

"Yeah." I curled into him and placed my head on his shoulder while staring at the sparkling ring. "It was Eric confirming numbers for his wedding. And giving me a heads up that Mona is coming too."

In two weeks, on Christmas Day, Eric was marrying the woman of his dreams, and I was supplying the alcohol for the event. However, it was the sister's impending arrival that rattled my nerves, more than the final head count.

"Mona?"

I sighed. "Mona is Lily's older sister. If Lily was considered a bad ass, Mona was on the opposite end of the spectrum, a goody-two-shoes to the core. She never coloured outside the lines, and apparently grew up to have the perfect life; a doting husband, a high-ranking job, everything she ever dreamed she'd get."

He rolled me over him, so he could gaze up into my eyes. "Why you sad?"

Yeah, why was I suddenly feeling like a deflated balloon?

I straddled my naked fiancé and placed my hands on his firm, rippled chest, grinding my hips. "As one who had her ear to the ground in terms of where the parties were going on, Mona enlisted in my help to find her sister and drag her back home."

"You her tour guide?" He chuckled.

"Yes and no. With Mona it's complicated. She's from a time in my life that I'd rather not focus on as she was so perfect, so put together. So motherly."

The giant diamond on my left hand sparkled under the beam of sunlight peeking in through the heavy drapes. I moved my hand and let the mini rainbows dance around the king-sized bed.

"Maybe she grow too?"

"I'd like to think so." My chin tucked into my chest.

Mona wasn't a bad person, on the contrary, she was someone I likely could've been friends with – had the right circumstances been there. As it was, because she was busy dragging Lily away from things, she saw more nasty stuff than she ever wanted – probably helped to keep her on the straight and narrow path. Sadly, I was a part of it, but that's how one stayed a breast of going-ons. I was sure those parties tainted her image of me too, and she saw me as just another one of Lily's wild gang, which wasn't true. Lily and I never ran in the same circles.

I just hoped she kept her lips sealed about the past. That shit didn't need to be brought up ever again.

"Guess I need to return you home." Antonio pumped his hips and gripped mine, rubbing me across his pelvis with enough pleasurably pressure to take my breath away.

"Yes... please." It was meant as a response to his statement, but the carnal waves inside crashed over me, ready for another round of sexy times.

He stopped moving. "When you tell your friends?"

"About our engagement?" My gaze fell to the ring.

He proposed with a gigantic rock, big enough to have cost more than my business and house combined. It was truly too much of a ring, but where we were now on the *Grand Divertmento*, weirdly enough, it wasn't out of place. However, for when I'm back home in Cheshire Bay, I had a smaller copy to wear – a ring that had once been his grandmother's. It was dainty and elegant and spoke softly about our impending nuptials whereas the true engagement ring I was to wear for the formal announcement and at any social gatherings outside of Cheshire Bay, screamed the news from the mountain tops.

"I'll tell them as soon as I get home."

Which was tomorrow evening, after our final full day of travel. We were expected in *Wharf Point* before nightfall.

"No, other."

Ah, the other. The loaded *other.*

As in when am I moving away from the only place I've called home?

He brushed the hairs off my face and rolled up to face me. "Most business is near my home."

"I know."

The past year he'd made several layovers with me, to the point where the locals had accepted him as one of them, but it wasn't permanent. He always needed to fly somewhere else as his home base was in Europe. He'd secured the Seattle location, but it wasn't the hub, and we both knew it. A giant sacrifice on my part was needed, especially now having accepted his strong hand in marriage.

"I'll tell them in the new year." I sealed the promise with a kiss.

I needed at least a few more weeks myself to come to terms with the idea of selling Amber's Ale and moving ten-thousand kilometers away. As much as I loved Antonio, and I truly did with all my heart and soul, this was a bigger step than getting married. But I could do it, and I wouldn't be alone. Maia, his sister, video chatted with us at least once a week, and his almost sister-in-law Genevieve, did the same. I already had a new family waiting to welcome me with open arms when I arrived full-time in the Mediterranean.

"I love you, Ember."

"I love you."

Beneath my hips, the swell of his love grew and pushed against me, ignoring all other thoughts. "I happy you be Mrs. Antonio Welsh."

I thrust my hips and connected with him, looking deep into his eyes. "Mrs. Amber Middleton-Welch, thank you." I made sure to pronounce my new last name accent free.

A broad smile filled his face. "Whatever name you want."

"For now, make me a woman." I tipped my head back, pushing my breasts into his face. "Then send me home to help my friends have their Christmas Day wedding so I can get ideas for ours."

More Fabulous Reads

For the most up-to-date listings, please check the website:
www.hmshander.com

Dear Reader

The Cheshire Bay series has been one of the most fun series I've written. I've enjoyed spending my time there, and drawing up the maps, creating the family trees, and picturing the completely fictional town. Why can't Cheshire Bay be real?

Keep reading the series and learn more about Lily, Cedar, Amber, Mona, Iris, Summer, Chloe, Erin, and Libby and their personal journeys to growth and love.

Would you like to be the first to know of upcoming releases, see the covers before anyone else, and just have all the insider information? Then you'll want to join my twice-a-month mailing list. Connect through my website – www.hmshander.com. I promise not to spam you, and I keep things fun with freebies and a scavenger hunt. Your time is valuable, and I appreciate how you've spent time reading my story (thank you for that!).

Finally, if you don't mind, I'd love a review on your favourite retailer site for Return to Cheshire Bay. It doesn't have to be long, even just as simple as "Antonio is my new book boyfriend" works. Reviews and ratings help me gain visibility, and as I'm sure you can tell, reviews are tough to come by. Thank you so much for spending time with me.

Yours,

H.M. Shander

acknowledgements

If one good thing came out of the pandemic in 2020, it was these books – I'm absolutely in love with this series and all the characters. They are each unique, but together, they form a beautiful series, if I do say so myself.

I'm in awe of being able to do what I love, and to fulfill my dream, but writing these thanks yous never gets easier. Never. Always afraid I'll miss someone, or a category will be left out. And then I wonder, does anyone even read these? I know as an author, I do, but I wonder if readers do? Anyways, writing a book for the most part, is a solo endeavor, but I could not have this ready for you to read if not for the cheerleading and support of some magnificent people in my life.

First – my Shander family, whom you may know on my social media platforms as Hubs, The Teen, and Little Dude. Thank you from the bottom of my heart for letting me pursue what I love doing, for something that allows me to transport myself to another time and place – the summer of 2020 was a particular straining time, and you gave me this golden escape into the pages. For that, I'll be forever grateful, and if this series does well, we're going to do something incredible. Like really big and fun. Thank you for cheerleading as I had a sale, and watching the numbers climb. Thank you for encouraging me to keep going and to chase my dreams, and for the nonstop coffees I sometimes needed when I was on a role. I love you all with my whole heart.

To my parents and in-laws and extended family – Thank you for your support, and encouraging your friends and family to give my books a try. Having you visit me at markets and book signings means the world. I have an amazing family, and every day I'm thankful to you all. Thanks for being you.

To my wonderfully dedicated alpha reader – Mandy. My trusted go-to writing pal, the one who reads the first cleaned up draft. Where would I be without your support and guidance? Probably still cowering in a corner. Your comments and feedback are vital to me. I never have to wait long, and before I know it, my inbox has a response, and 99% of the time, your advice is bang on. I'm so glad we're in this business together, and you know I'm your biggest fan and cheerleader! You're going to go big, and I'm tagging along on the ride. You deserve the very best.

To my critique partner – Josephine. Thank you for spending your free time reading my words and pointing out what didn't make sense and what needed to be expanded on. How many times did I redo that opening chapter in Return? LOL, and Awake? You had your work cut out with that, eh? But, as always, your insight was invaluable, and the stories are better with your touch! Thank you.

To my beta readers – Shauna, Melissa, and Dawn. Thank you for cheering for the good, highlighting the bad, and letting me know what worked and what needed more explanation. Your feedback and insight are a gift I cherish.

To my cover designer – Eleanor. Great job! I'm super thrilled with how well all the covers turned out, including the special edition print cover! I simple adore all of them and can't stop staring! I'm so blessed to have discovered your talents, and I look forward to many more covers designed by you.

To my editor – Irina. Thanks for your dedication to fixing my errors and highlighting the inconsistencies. I think I'm getting better, right? At least it's not the same corrections every time. Heh-heh.

If I missed you, it certainly wasn't intentional. I know I couldn't be where I am without the help of so many others. Thank you! And thank you for reading and making it all the way to the end. You all rock.

about the author

USA TODAY bestselling author H.M. Shander is a star-gazing, romantic at heart who once attended Space Camp and wanted to pilot the space shuttle, not just any STS – specifically Columbia. However, the only shuttle she operates in her real world is the #momtaxi; a reliable electric car that transports her two kids to school and various sporting events. When she's not commandeering Elektra, you can find the elementary school librarian surrounded by classes of children as she reads the best storybooks in multiple voices. After she's tucked her endearing kids into bed and kissed her trophy husband goodnight, she moonlights as a contemporary romance novelist; the writer of sassy heroines and sweet, swoon-worthy heroes who find love in the darkest of places.

If you want to know when her next heart-filled journey is coming out, you can follow her on Twitter (@HM_Shander), Facebook (hmshander), or check out her website at www.hmshander.com.

Thanks for reading– all the way to the very end.

www.ingramcontent.com/pod-product-compliance
Lightning Source LLC
Chambersburg PA
CBHW050822180626
46814CB00004B/1420